Operation Nativity

To my agent, Sam Copeland, this story wouldn't be
what it is without you.

This edition first published in the UK in 2023 by Usborne Publishing Limited,
Usborne House, 83-85 Saffron Hill, London EC1N 8RT, England. usborne.com

Usborne Verlag, Usborne Publishing Limited, Prüfeninger Str. 20,
93049 Regensburg, Deutschland, VK Nr. 17560

First published 2022. Text copyright © Jenny Pearson, 2022

Cover and inside illustrations by Katie Kear © Usborne Publishing Limited, 2022

Typography by Thy Bui © Usborne Publishing Limited, 2022

Author name typography by Sarah Coleman © Usborne Publishing Limited, 2022

The right of Jenny Pearson to be identified as the author of this work has been
asserted by her in accordance with the Copyright, Designs and Patents Act, 1988.

The name Usborne and the Balloon logo are Trade Marks of
Usborne Publishing Limited.

A CIP catalogue record for this book is available from the British Library.

JFMAMJ ASOND/23 ISBN 9781801315111 7688/2

Printed and bound using 100% renewable electricity at CPI Group (UK) Ltd CR0 4YY.

MIX
Paper | Supporting
responsible forestry
FSC® C171272

Operation Nativity

JENNY PEARSON

Illustrations by Katie Kear

USBORNE

The First Noel at Barlington Hall

I'm going to tell you the story about the birth of the baby Jesus. You might have heard about it from your teachers at school. You may have been in a nativity play yourself, with either tinsel on your head or a fake beard strapped to your face, so I'm sure you know the gist – Mary, Joseph, donkey, journey from Nazareth to Bethlehem. Well, that part is spot on the money.

The bit that they won't have told you about is the accidental detour Mary and Joseph took to Chipping Bottom, a pretty and characterful village in Hampshire, which came about thanks to a less-than-professional spot of angeling.

Yes, that says *angeling* not angling – there is no fishing involved in the story of the birth of Jesus Christ. There is, however, a bit of a bump in the journey thanks to the Angel Gabriel messing things up ever so *slightly*.

And when I say ever so *slightly*, I really mean ever so *massively*. But you have to remember, back then, he hadn't been in the job that long. It was an awful lot of pressure – announcing the arrival of the actual Jesus Christ – and let's just say he got a bit carried away. He couldn't have known that the explosion of light he came down to Earth in would be so powerful that it would transport Mary, Joseph, Balthazar the wise man, a shepherd named Steve *and* himself not only to another place (Chipping Bottom) but to another time (last December).

But how do *I* know all this?

Good question.

And the answer is because I. WAS. THERE!

Big claim, I know. You are well within your rights to say, *Oscar, are you possibly a teensy-lot confused? You were most certainly not present at the birth of Jesus Christ Our Lord, and the Angel Gabriel most definitely did not mess things up.* But I'd say this: people will always make big claims and it's up to you to choose whether to believe them or not.

For example, I do not believe Dad was beamed up to Kepler-452b by some aliens, like he told Mum that time he came home late from the rugby. I also suspect Tyronne in my class was lying when he said that when he was eight, Santa Claus woke him up and took him on his round-the-world delivery flight because he'd been the best-behaved boy on the planet. And there is no way the chocolate Santa that I had been saving in the fridge vanished in a puff of smoke one night like Mum tried to get me to believe. There was no evidence to support any of those claims.

But there is also no evidence I can show to convince you that I was around when Jesus was about to be born. Other than a two-thousand-year-old donkey at Lady Asster's donkey sanctuary. But, to be honest, Mary's donkey looks pretty much the same as all the others. Even I struggle to tell him and his stablemate Zipper apart – and I spent quite a few hours plodding through the countryside on the back of Mary's donkey.

So really, all I can do is tell you my story and all you can do is listen, if you want to, and then decide if you think it's true. Hopefully, I'll be more convincing than Tyronne at least. I mean, nobody could be *that* good, and definitely not Tyronne. But I suppose it doesn't really matter if I can convince you or not. People will always believe different things and I actually think that's okay.

For example, I believed Christmas was important for two reasons. Number one: presents. And number two: it was the day my parents met. And if there was no Christmas, then they might not have met, and then they wouldn't have had me. And that would be an *actual* tragedy.

But now, after everything, I truly believe there are more important things than presents. And more important things than me.

Even my family believe different things about what happened. Like my grandmother – she's a bit of a traditionalist when it comes to Christmas. She loves the nativity story and she'd never believe that the Virgin Mary and Joseph ended up in Chipping Bottom, even if she did bump into them in the post office and not realize.

Whereas my little sister Molly...let's just say she's the open-minded type. She really will believe *anything* you tell her, without question. As her school report said, *her imagination knows no bounds.* She's convinced she can speak to animals and she's certain that one day wings will sprout from her shoulder blades. But then she's only five-and-a-bit.

I suppose that if Molly wasn't the way she is, none of what happened last Christmas would have happened. But after we had both seen something crash-land in the field behind our grandparents' house, she was the one who convinced *me* that it might be something spectacular and we should go and check it out.

The only reason we were even there was because we'd received a very fancy invitation in the post from Barlington Hall – a summons to head back to my dad's family home for Christmas. Which, if you think about it, is a little bit like the summons Mary and Joseph were given to travel to Bethlehem by Emperor Augustus. I'm not saying Grandmother is *exactly* like a Roman Emperor – but there are a few similarities.

Anyway, if we hadn't gone to Barlington for Christmas and if we hadn't very bravely ventured out into the field that night, I don't think it's too big-headed to say that basically Christmas would have been destroyed. Well, actually it would have never existed in the first place.

9

But I don't think there's a word for destroying something that never existed. So, if you do believe everything I'm about to tell you, you can thank me for saving Christmas later.

Peace on Earth?

(Not at ours, with all the Pa-rum-pum-pum-pumping!)

I don't know why, but I had a feeling that Christmas was going to be a bit different to normal as soon as the invitation arrived. Usually, we just have Mum's mum, Granny Roberts, over, but she'd booked a cruise around the Canary Islands with her friend, Irene, who she met on the number 67 bus. They were starting at Santa Cruz in Tenerife and ending in Las Palmas in Gran Canaria. Molly *really* wanted to go with them, but when we explained that they weren't visiting islands full of little yellow tweety-birds and that Father Christmas did not live in Tenerife, she changed her mind.

I was actually excited to be doing something different

for a change. I love Granny Roberts, but I can't say I was too worried about not spending Christmas with her. No offence, but she doesn't really add that much to the day. See, she doesn't have a lot of stamina for fun, what with her being a-gazillion-and-one years old. Every year, Mum tells her to go steady on the Buck's Fizz, but Granny Roberts doesn't listen. She spends the morning grabbing hold of me and my sister Molly and squeezing our faces while telling us we're her favourite grandkids. I mean, that's nice, but even Molly knows that as we're her *only* grandkids, there's no actual competition.

Sometimes, Granny Roberts will suddenly break into a very warbly version of "Deck the Halls" and Dad will say, "Cathy, your mother has peaked too early again," and Mum will say, "She's fine, Christopher, let her be!" But she'll always fall asleep around three o'clock.

This one year, she slumped down on top of the Monopoly board just as Dad had landed on my Park Lane where I had two hotels! That took some forgiving, I'll tell you. Another time she spent the entire afternoon snoring and farting in front of the TV. It was funny at first – I mean, who doesn't find an unconscious old lady trumpeting along to the Queen's Speech hilarious? But when the room became so unbelievably stinky that I couldn't watch *Home Alone* without my T-shirt over my nose, I began to question Mum and Dad's wisdom in allowing her to have a third helping of sprouts. And then, the year before last, she almost didn't even make it through the meal! She nearly nodded off in her gravy and sausage-meat stuffing. Really, I think if you're a guest at someone's house, you should bring a bit more Christmas spirit with you.

Mind you, there's Christmas spirit and then there's an angel with an eye-blindingly bright halo in your downstairs toilet.

But at the time, I didn't think it was possible to have too much Christmas spirit, so when an invitation to spend Christmas at Barlington Hall with Dad's side of the family, the Cuthbert-Andersons, turned up, I jumped at the chance.

The invite was very fancy, with grand-looking handwriting on the front, and sealed with a red blobby wax thing of the family crest. Oh yeah, Dad's side of the family are super rich. Old money, Granny Roberts says – whatever that is.

My rich grandparents live on a huge country estate

in Hampshire. Molly says Barlington Hall is majestiful, which isn't a real word, but is spot on as descriptions go, because Barlington Hall is both majestic and wonderful.

The house itself is set in acres of land and you have to make your way through these huge iron gates with lions on them and head up a really long driveway before you even get to the front door! There are so many massive rooms, including a library, two kitchens, loads of bathrooms, spare sitting rooms and a ballroom! Half of it isn't even used because it is so expensive to look after. Imagine that! Having a bit of your house that you never even go in.

The closed-off wing was actually very useful though – for storing lost angels and wise men. But more about that later.

We usually visit Barlington Hall in summer, for a week of the school holidays. Mum is never that thrilled when we go. She says she and my grandmother are very different people, which is a fair statement. I love it there though. We spend our time climbing the best trees you'll ever find to climb and fishing for minnows down in the stream at the bottom of one of the fields. One year we even built a chicken run with Grandfather. It's also where Dad taught me to ride a bike and where we lost Molly for almost an hour during the most epic game of hide-and-seek. But we'd never been there for Christmas before. I thought that was because we had to look after Granny Roberts, but I soon realized there was more to it than that.

When the invitation arrived in the post that morning, I immediately started imagining Barlington Hall at wintertime, with its fireplaces lit and the house decorated all festively. I knew that a Christmas there would be absolutely majestiful, and I just had this feeling that it was going to be way more exciting than our regular Christmases.

Obviously, I had no idea just *how* much more exciting it would be and that I would meet some very important people and be involved in saving Christmas and all it stands for. I don't think anybody, even Molly, could have had the imagination to predict *that* was about to go down.

But the first thing I needed to do was get Mum on board with the whole Barlington trip and I realized that might be tricky when she picked up the invitation from the doormat, took one look at it and said, "Oh no. No, no, no! Not the family nativity!"

Now, of course I'd heard stories about the family nativity – it's some big production that Grandmother puts on in her local church. The first ever one was in nineteen-twenty-something and was started by my great-great-great-grandmother, Lady Cordelia Cuthbert-Anderson, who was a bit of a character by all accounts. Her shows were known to be quite the spectacle. Apparently, you can still see scorch marks on the altar where Cordelia let off an indoor firework to announce the arrival of the Angel Gabriel in the 1929 production.

Generation after generation of Cuthbert-Andersons have prided themselves on putting on a grand show in the village, trying to make each performance better than the last.

I thought it sounded like a lot of fun, but Molly and I had never been involved because Mum and Dad always said something about *liking to do our own thing at Christmas*. But I got a strong suspicion we might not have been told the full story when Mum stood there glaring at that invitation, muttering, "No, no, no, I said never again, not after the last time…" And then she bellowed up the stairs to Dad, "CHRISTOPHER! WE HAVE A PROBLEM!"

O Come, All Ye Faithful

(because Grandmother demands it)

On the morning the invite arrived in the post, Molly ran to the door, shouting, "POSSSSSST!" I dropped my games controller and raced out to see if I could beat her to it. There's always a bit of a bundle between us to see who can get there first, even though Mum tells us off for it.

Molly pointed at me with her foam cutlass. "Back off, Osky! It's MINE!"

She was dressed in one of what our family calls her "casual day outfits". Molly point-blank refuses to wear normal clothes. Today she was wearing the bottom part of her Tin Man costume, the top part of a pirate outfit and her Christmas reindeer bopper headband.

I tried to dodge round her, but she waggled her weapon in my face and did a big pirately "ARGGGH!".

That's when Mum swooped in, gasped as she realized what was in the envelope and then deafened us both by shouting, "CHRISTOPHER! WE HAVE A PROBLEM!"

Clearly, this wasn't usual post.

Molly started to yank on Mum's top. "Is it post for me?"

"No, darling... CHRISTOPHER, would you get down here?"

Molly stuck out her lip. "I never get post."

"That's because you're only five," I said.

"Lucky you, I don't think I want this post, Molly-pops." Mum turned the letter over in her hands, then closed her eyes and whispered what sounded a bit like a prayer.

Dad came down the stairs. "What is it, love?"

"Is it bad-bill post?" Molly asked.

"I fear it's worse than that, darling. It's from Barlington Hall," Mum said, pulling the cord of her dressing gown tighter. She looked at Dad. "It's the Christmas invite from your mother. I presume you know

something about this? You told them, didn't you, that we don't have my mother for Christmas this year!"

"Ah, yes, I probably need to talk to you about that."

"Yes, you probably do. I thought we'd made our feelings clear on this. You promised I'd never have to take part in the family nativity ever again!"

"Come on, love, it's not *that* bad," Dad said, sounding wholly unconvincing.

"Christopher," Mum seethed, "your mother had me dangling from the church balcony dressed up in a gold leotard pretending to be a star!"

"And a very lovely star you made too!"

"Until the rope came loose! And what about the time I was put in charge of Morris?"

"Who's Morris?" I asked.

"A sheep," Dad said.

"I think you'll find he was a ram! I had bruises for weeks after he went on that rampage! And if that's not enough to remind you of how horrendous the whole thing is, let's not forget your mother's approach to directing 'her actors'!"

Dad looked at me and said, "Your grandmother can get a little passionate."

"Passionate!" Mum yelled. "Christopher, she's a monster. No – no way is this happening." She then headed off down the hallway, muttering something about how she must have done something really bad in a past life to get letters from Lady Lucifer.

We followed her into the kitchen, and I sat down at the table which was covered with all Mum's cake tins. She's gone part-time at the pensions company so she can spend more time learning to bake professionally. She'd had a go at stollen that week, and I reckon by the sixth attempt you would definitely think it was the marzipanny-fruity Christmas loaf from Germany and not a crunchy baguette from France.

Mum stuck the kettle on and Dad sat down at the table.

I could tell it was going to be one of *those* adult conversations, because Mum got rid of Molly by sending her off with her advent calendar to find the next window. They couldn't trick me though. I was going to stick around for this one.

Molly disappeared into the sitting room and I heard her start up her battery-powered lightsaber and begin launching her daily attack on her Sylvanian family collection.

"Can I have a look?" I asked, grabbing the invitation from the table. "Who's Lady Lucifer? Grandmother?"

"Nobody. You never heard that, understand?" Mum said, then chucked teabags into two mugs. "Hot chocolate, Oscar?"

"Yes please," I said, turning the invitation around in my hands. The paper was thick and creamy in colour, with gold edging. It was covered with Grandmother's fancy calligraphy writing, which told us we had been cordially invited to Barlington Hall for the one hundredth Cuthbert-Anderson Christmas nativity. I have to say, I was sold on the idea immediately. Who doesn't want to be cordially invited somewhere?

"Has it really come around again already? It can't be three years." Mum sighed.

"I'm afraid so," Dad said.

Mum poured the hot water into the mugs, then squirted some whippy cream on my hot chocolate.

"I think the family nativity sounds fun. Let's do it!" I said, because if there was a chance I'd get to see my mum dangling from a harness in a shiny outfit, I did not want to miss that.

Mum put her cup down, closed her eyes, then shook

her head as though she was trying to forget some terrible memory – could have been the church balcony-dangling, but maybe it was the ram-butting, who knows?

"That," Mum said in a slightly unnerving voice, "is because you've never been involved."

I said, "But it's a family tradition and I am part of the Cuthbert-Anderson family, so I want to be a part of it and I'm glad we've received an invitation."

"*Summons* more like," Mum said.

"Your grandmother does tend to get quite wrapped up in the whole thing," Dad said, then swallowed hard.

"That's one way of putting it," Mum said. "You may have grasped that your grandmother is quite a ferocious dictator."

"She means director," Dad said to me.

"Do I? The first year I did it, after having met your father, I was demoted to a non-speaking part – a palm tree, would you believe? All because I could not portray an angel 'authentically'. Oh, Christopher, she'll be even worse if it's a hundredth celebration! You know how she gets!"

I thought about Grandmother Cuthbert-Anderson and, sure, she does have lots of rules – about where we sit at dinner and the order of cutlery, for example. And yes, she was a big one for manners, but I couldn't imagine that she could be as bad as Mum was making out. And she was family after all. Dad says you just have to accept family and love them for who they are, and I reckon he's right about that, even if they do go a bit extra about a nativity play.

Mum passed Dad and me our mugs and sighed. "It's all quite an..."

"Experience?" I suggested.

"Ordeal," she said, then swallowed hard.

Frankly, she was starting to sound a bit melodramatic. An ordeal to me is accidentally getting blasted into space on a pogo stick, or being attacked by a herd of sealions, or forgetting to wear underpants to school on a PE day.

An ordeal was *not* a family nativity play.

Or so I thought...but then I had no clue as to what the Angel Gabriel was about to do two thousand years ago and what I'd have to do to fix it.

I began lapping up the whippy cream. "Sounds alright to me," I said, taking a big slurp. "I don't understand why you don't want to go."

Mum sat herself down on the kitchen worktop. "We just prefer doing Christmas *our way*."

24

"It's nice to keep it as just us. Christmas Day is when your mother and I met, which makes it extra special," Dad said, smiling at Mum.

I groaned inwardly – they were going to tell the how-they-met story again.

"Yes, it's the day you rolled up to my door dressed as an elf while carol-singing – if you can call it singing."

"I had no elf-control and asked your mother out immediately."

"Dad, that joke wasn't funny the first time you told it."

"Anyway," Mum continued, "we usually have Granny Roberts to think about."

"Well, she's off to the Canaries, so I think this year we should change things up!" I said.

"Can't we think of another reason not to go?" Mum asked. "We've always managed to come up with some excuse."

"What excuses?" I asked.

"We can't always use Granny Roberts, so usually, we find another reason to avoid all the family...*drama*. Last time we said we couldn't go because you'd had your tonsils out. The time before that, it was your grommets," Dad said.

"Oh, Christopher, I really hoped that they'd got the picture that we're not keen," Mum said. Then she turned to me. "I don't suppose you have any more body parts we could have removed so we don't have to attend?"

"How's your appendix feeling?" Dad said and gave me a wink.

"My appendix is fine," I said. I was not completely clear on what an appendix was, but I did not like what he was insinuating.

Mum sighed and said, "Shame," in a way that sounded like she actually was disappointed about my appendix being fit-for-purpose.

"Hang on! You didn't make me have my tonsils out so we didn't have to do this nativity thing, did you?"

"No!" Mum said, sounding a little too flustered for my liking.

"Hmmm." I gave them both a look.

"I suppose there's always Molly. She hasn't had her tonsils out yet," Dad said. Then he grinned at me. "That is, if you're one hundred per cent sure your appendix is feeling A-okay. Are you sure there are no little twinges?"

I gasped and Mum laughed and threw a tea towel at Dad.

"No," I said, "and even if it was twinging I wouldn't tell you, because I think we should go! I like the idea of some festive family tra-la-la-ing around the Christmas tree! I bet the tree at Barlington will be massive! And Grandfather and Grandmother are bound to decorate the place all festive and fancy – it will feel extra Christmassy there!"

Mum frowned and turned to Dad. "Christopher, I do not think we can harvest any more body parts from our children to get out of it this year. You'll just have to say a polite 'Thank you, but no thank you.' Make it clear this time."

Dad stopped smiling and for a moment I didn't recognize the look on his face. He suddenly looked very small – a bit like a kid. Well, a stubbly, slightly wrinkled kid, but you get what I'm trying to say. "Normally, I would – you know how I feel about the whole Barlington Hall Christmas *thing* – but this year, I really think we ought to go. It's my dad, see…" He took a big swallow of his tea and Mum and I looked at each other while we waited for him to continue. "He's not well. James called yesterday – they're all getting the ferry over for it this year. Camilla and Patryk are going too."

James is my dad's brother. He's married to my Aunty Marigold. They both work in something financy and have twins called Hugo and Fenella. I didn't know my cousins *that* well. They live in Jersey, which is closer to France than us. We used to see them at Barlington in the summer holidays, but we hadn't overlapped for the last couple of years so I hadn't seen them since I was about eight.

Camilla is my dad's little sister and Uncle Patryk is her husband. Aunty Camilla used to write a column in a magazine telling everybody what it was like being a single girl in London, but then she met Uncle Patryk and she couldn't do that any more. Since then she's been writing about pregnancy and soft furnishings, according to Mum. I don't really know what soft furnishings are, or what she's got against hard ones.

"Poor Reginald. It's not gout again, is it?" Mum asked.

I know what gout is because of *Horrible Histories*. Henry VIII had it a lot. It's when your joints get sore and painful because you eat too many boar heads and drink too much wine.

"It's a bit worse than gout," Dad said very quietly and looked at the floor. "A lot worse, Cathy." Then he looked at me. "Oscar, maybe you shouldn't be here for this, it might upset you."

I put my hot chocolate down. "Is Grandfather sick? If he is, I want to know. I'm almost twelve, that's practically a teenager. I can handle it."

Dad looked at Mum and she nodded.

"Yes, he is rather ill," Dad said.

"Is it bad?" I said quietly.

"I'm afraid so, champ. And I know how difficult you find the nativity, Cathy, and usually I wouldn't ask, but I think this may be the last time..."

"Right, goodness," Mum said, putting her mug down on the draining board. She slid off the worktop and onto her feet. Then she turned the tap on full blast and started filling the washing-up bowl. Mum has a habit of *doing things* when she doesn't know what to do.

"Goodness, right, goodness, of course, of course, right," she repeated as she gave some innocent plates quite an aggressive cleaning.

I sat there, thinking about my grandfather. I don't see him nearly as much as I'd like because we live three hundred miles away in Middlesbrough. We moved here for Dad's job at the biotech and pharmaceuticals company, just after I was born. To begin with, apparently my grandparents were disappointed he didn't want to take on the responsibility of living in Barlington, although they've got over it now. I heard Dad talking about it with Mum once. He said that he didn't want the "burden of being a Cuthbert-Anderson and all that that entails". I didn't really know what that meant, to be honest. I failed to see how living in an enormo house could be a burden – all those rooms to run around in and a huge garden to play in. But there had to be something in it, because my Uncle James and Auntie Camilla didn't want to live at Barlington either.

Anyway, with us in Middlesbrough and my grandparents in Hampshire, it's not like we've ever been able to just pop round. We Zoom them every other weekend, but neither him nor Grandmother are that great with technology. We often end up having conversations with their bellies and they spend a lot of time saying, "Can you hear us? We can't hear you!" but I like our chats. Grandfather is one of those people who seem to be made up of stories. You know how *stuff* just happens to some people? Well, he's one of *them*.

Thinking about it now, I guess I am too.

But back to Grandfather. This one time, he got knocked off his horse by a low-flying pheasant. And one wintry February evening, he somehow managed to set fire to his pyjamas by bending over to warm his bum by the fire, and had to run outside and sit in the snow to put them out. And this one time, when we were there for the summer holidays, he let me drive the Land Rover and Mum went ballistic and called him a reckless old fish because I was only six and six-year-olds aren't really supposed to drive Land Rovers. I don't know where the fish bit came from. I think she was overwrought with emotion at seeing her son crash into the side of the house and it was the first thing that came out of her mouth.

Anyway, my grandfather – or Lord Cuthbert-Anderson, to give him his full title – really is quite a lot of fun. I know the Lord part might make you think that he's a bit stuffy, but he definitely isn't. I'm not even sure what a Lord does, other than dress up and go to occasional fancy dinners. To me, he's just my grandfather, and a really very brilliant one.

I suddenly felt very, very sad and very, very determined that a Christmas at Barlington Hall was, for so many reasons, absolutely what we had to do.

I turned to Mum. "Go on, I think we should do this nativity thing and spend Christmas at Barlington. Granny Roberts isn't with us this year, so really, what else are we going to do? And Grandfather Cuthbert-Anderson is my only grandad, and I would very much like to see him before the thing that is worse than gout gets him. It is Christmas, after all. I say, let the family festive fun begin! What's the worst that can happen?"

Quite a lot as it turned out, but how was I to know that the Angel Gabriel was about to make such a monumental mistake?

"Of course we'll go," Mum said. "Absolutely."

Dad walked over and gave her a hug. "You never know, love, we might even enjoy it."

Molly staggered into the kitchen at that moment, her face smeared with chocolate. Under her arm was a clearly ransacked advent calendar – every window of the Santa-and-his-reindeers scene was open. She did a massive burp, said, "I feel a bit icky-poos," then promptly threw up on the kitchen lino.

I didn't think much of it at the time, but Mum clearly saw it as some sort of sign as to how the holiday season would pan out. Mums are weirdly psychic like that.

Because she closed her eyes and said very quietly, "And so it begins." Like Molly puking was some proof that we were heading towards a Christmas catastrophe.

Which, as it so happens, was remarkably close to the truth.

It's beginning to look a lot like

Mum should have driven

Grandmother Cuthbert-Anderson had insisted we arrive by the twentieth of December at *the absolute latest*, as she had drawn up a strict rehearsal schedule for which it was essential that we were present. Mum had turned very white when she read that email.

So that Friday, the twentieth of December, we set off in Colin our camper van after tea, because it is easier to drive at night when Molly is asleep. This is because, number one, it means we don't have to listen to her singing "There's a hole in my bucket" for hours on end, and two, we also don't have to stop every five minutes for her to do a wee.

Mum made me sit with a Christmas cake in my lap that was so heavy it made my legs go numb. My tingly toes were not helped by the fact that the journey took a little longer than it should have. Dad had programmed the wrong Hampshire into the satnav and we headed off to Hampshire County in Massachusetts, until Mum spotted that the journey was 3,229 miles, which seemed a wee bit lengthy. He really is rubbish at directions.

After that, Dad decided to ignore the satnav altogether. We ended up going a way he later described as the "picturesque route" and which Mum said was a "tour through the back end of beyond" and an hour and a half of her life that she would never get back.

It was midway through our tour of the back end of beyond that I realized I'd left my phone on my bedside table. I tried to persuade them to go back for it, but they were having none of it because it would, apparently, be a good lesson for me to learn to do without it. I tried to show them that they were wrong about that by sulking for the rest of the journey, which they seemed to find amusing.

When we arrived at Barlington Hall, my legs were completely asleep and my tongue was a bit sore from all the super-sour candy canes I'd been sucking. But I quickly forgot about my discomfort when we passed through those big gates and drove up the long, sweeping drive towards the house. The driveway is lined with these impressively tall trees which Dad had once told me were cedars. As we pulled up outside, we found Grandfather tangled up in a string of Christmas lights at the top of a stepladder.

"Is that my father? At this hour? What's the silly old fool up to now?" Dad said, turning off the ignition and jumping out of Colin.

I climbed out after him, put the Christmas cake on the ground next to the van and brushed off the Skips and other food debris which had become welded between my legs during the journey.

"Hurrah!" my grandfather said. "The weary travellers have arrived at long last."

I realized I did feel quite weary when he said that. Granted, it was no sixty-five mile trek on the back of a donkey along a dusty road, but listening to my parents bicker and having no phone for entertainment was also quite a trial.

"Dad, what are you doing up there at this time of

night and in your condition?" Dad said, striding up to the front steps.

"Your mother wanted these up for your arrival. But it would appear that one has failed on that front. Usually Geoffrey the gardener does this, but your mother had him loading the trailer with logs for the fire all day and I only remembered the lights when the ten o'clock news came on. Ah, young Oscar, would you see if you can locate the end? I'm afraid I'm in a dreadful pickle."

"Dad, would you please get down before you electrocute yourself or worse! I'll put up the lights tomorrow."

"But your mother—"

"She will just have to wait – now come here." Dad offered his hand and my grandfather took it and unsteadily made his way down the ladder.

"Here's the end," I said.

"Oh, bravo, Oscar!" Grandfather said. "Now if you wouldn't mind unravelling me."

I pulled on the end of the wire and he spun around like a prima ballerina in a tweed flat cap until he was freed. Right then, seeing him like that, I wondered if Dad had got it all wrong about him being ill. He looked really

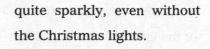

quite sparkly, even without the Christmas lights.

Mum came up to the front steps, carrying a sleeping Molly in her arms.

"Goodness me," Grandfather said, "what on the Lord's sweet Earth is that child wearing?"

"It's a Gruffalo onesie," I said.

"Well I never! A Gruffalo, you say? What a thing!" He did a big chortly laugh that Santa himself would be proud of. Then he placed his hand on Mum's shoulder and, looking super sincere, said, "Cathy, you are a delight for the eyes. It has been far too long!"

"It's good to see you too, Reginald," Mum said, and although she was smiling, she couldn't keep the sadness out of her voice.

"Come now, come now." My grandfather stepped out of the light string that had fallen in a nest around his feet and turned towards the front door. "These children must be off to bed at once, your mother has a full day of activities planned tomorrow. I believe Marigold and James are arriving with their lot before lunch and Camilla and Patryk are due in time for supper."

So to recap, James is my dad's older brother and Marigold is his wife. They are the ones with the twins, Hugo and Fenella. Camilla is my dad's younger sister. She's married to Patryk. Patryk's family live in Poland but he decided to move here permanently when his career took off. He's an architect and he's in charge of a whole company that builds great big skyscrapers in London. They were expecting their first kid any day.

My grandfather pushed open the huge front doors and said, with a very satisfying amount of drama in his voice, "Welcome to Christmas at Barlington."

And I said, "Thank you very much." And then I stepped inside and said, "Wow!"

You cannot fail to be impressed by the entrance hall of Barlington. It is enormous. There's a huge twinkling chandelier hanging from a very high ceiling, and a table holding a giant vase with the most enormous flower arrangement you'll ever see. It was filled with all red and white flowers and green leaves. It was like someone had grown Christmas and popped it in a fancy pot to display.

"Blimey, I don't think there are enough flowers in our whole garden to fill that vase," I said. "Mind you, we don't have that many in our garden at all, because, according to Dad, 'it's a place where plants go to die'."

"I don't think I ever said that," Dad said, looking nervously over at Mum.

"Yeah, you did. That time we all went round B&Q garden centre – you even did pretend plant voices whenever Mum went near them, remember? *Don't pick me, I'm too young to die. I'm only a tiny baby sapling!*"

"I am an excellent gardener," Mum said, but we all knew that was a lie.

"Mum, you even managed to kill a plastic plant once." I turned to relay the story to my grandfather. "She set fire to it with a candle. I'd even told her what the fireman who came to our school assembly said about leaving flames unattended, but she must have forgotten about that when she was on the phone arguing with someone from a delivery company.

"She was too busy telling them that she'd delivered both her children quicker, to notice that the huge plastic palm thing had caught alight."

"Yes, *thank you*, Oscar," Mum said, a little hotly. It wasn't a genuine *thank you*, just the way she tells me to be quiet sometimes.

The vase wasn't the only impressive thing about the hallway. By the table was a giant Christmas tree decorated in red and gold, which Mum would say was very tasteful but I would say was somewhat lacking. I think Christmas trees are way better when they have all the colours on them. I'm talking pink, orange, red, gold, blue, luminous yellow – the lot. And tinsel. Barlington Hall's Christmas tree might have been large, but it didn't have any tinsel.

Behind the tree, two staircases descended from the upper landing.

A Christmassy garland of green leaves and red bows weaved in and out of the banisters. I'd have to get that off at some point. Those banisters were made to be slid down, but decorative holly up the bum would ruin anyone's Christmas. As I started planning my launch point, I had a sudden memory of Grandfather careering down them one summer holiday, shouting "Onwards, to battle we go, Sir Oscar!" It made me smile and I was convinced, once again, that Christmas at Barlington was really going to be quite excellent.

Grandfather clapped his hands. "Right, let's not stand around here all evening. Christopher, your mother is in the drawing room. She wishes to cast eyes on the children before they retire for the evening." Grandfather looked at Molly, who was still asleep and clinging to Mum like a koala. "Although perhaps one should forewarn her that her granddaughter is dressed as a Gruffalo. She is not one for surprises after eight o'clock in the evening."

"I'm sure it will be fine," Dad said.

Mum raised an eyebrow, which suggested she wasn't as completely sure as Dad.

We followed Grandfather through the high-ceilinged

hallways, past all the old paintings of fancy-looking folk in frilly clothes, to the drawing room. My grandmother was perched on a chair, reading a book next to a roaring fire, while classical music played quietly in the background. She had a tartan blanket draped over her legs and was wearing a high buttoned blouse under a navy cardigan.

She put down her book as we entered, then took off her reading glasses, letting them dangle from a string around her neck.

"They have arrived," Grandfather announced.

"Yes, I see," my grandmother said. "Later than we had agreed, but I suppose one must be grateful that you are here at all."

"Hello, Mother," Dad said. "We did manage to make it for the twentieth!"

"Just." She turned her cheek towards him and Dad walked over to her and gave it a kiss.

She then looked at me. "Oscar Charles, I haven't seen you since last summer, come closer to me, so I may inspect you."

I don't know why she used my middle name. I suppose it's good that someone uses it, it's just sitting there doing nothing most of the time.

"You look a little thin," she said, then looked at my mum. "Tell me, Catherine, is this child undernourished?"

I lifted up my jumper and stared down at my tummy. It looked alright to me. I pushed it out and sucked it back in a few times. The first time was to check its size, but the others were really just for my own amusement. Sure, I wasn't about to win any bodybuilding competitions, but I wouldn't say I was thin.

"He's perfectly healthy," Mum said, hoicking Molly up higher onto her hips.

"Yup," I agreed. "Not even a twinge from my appendix," I said, patting roughly where I thought my appendix would be, somewhere around my right nipple.

My grandmother frowned, looked me up and down and said, "What an extraordinary thing to say."

I said, "Thank you," because I had never been told I'd said anything extraordinary before.

Then she said, "Say hello to your grandmother properly, please," and turned her cheek to me.

I wasn't sure what she meant by a *proper hello*, but I imagined she wanted a little more enthusiasm, so I flung my arms wide and half-sang, half-spoke, "HELLO, GRANDMOTHER!" quite impressively loudly.

She turned to look at my dad and said, "Christopher, is this child quite sane? Or is it that his social etiquette has suffered in the months since you last visited? I imagine an over-dependency on video games is to blame."

"He's perfectly sane," Mum interjected. "And his screen time is closely monitored."

"What are you talking about?" I said, because I was completely lost at this point.

"Basically, your grandmother would like a kiss," Dad explained.

I'd hoped to avoid this and I considered saying, *I'd like an Xbox and a sightseeing trip round the moon, but we don't always get what we want, old lady – these lips aren't kissing anything.* But something told me that wouldn't go down brilliantly.

My grandmother turned her cheek towards me again.

I stood there looking at it for a while. It resembled a dried apricot – one that had been dusted with white powder. I imagined I was a teeny-tiny person on a snow mobile driving up and down her cheek grooves. I really didn't want to put my lips anywhere near her face, but when I looked at Dad for support he just nodded, so I did a really quick peck and stepped back, relieved to have got it over with.

"I'm afraid Molly is fast asleep, I should probably get her into bed," Mum said.

"Good Lord, is that a child you are carrying?" my grandmother spluttered. "I believed it to be some sort of large stuffed animal. Why on Earth is she dressed like that?"

"It's a Gruffalo onesie," I said. "She likes to wear it at night because she thinks it scares the monsters away. I'm not sure what monsters. Maybe the bogeyman... probably not the Loch Ness one, as that's in a loch somewhere in Scotland...possibly gremlins. I'm not one hundred per cent on that, she was a bit vague when I asked her about it."

"A Gruffalo? A onesie? Monsters?" my grandmother said, like they were the most peculiar words to ever pass her lips. "Christopher, I do wonder as to how you are bringing these children up. All-in-one attire really has no business on a Cuthbert-Anderson."

"We're Andersons," Mum said.

"And he's brung us up just fine," I said, and pushed my stomach out as far as I could to show that I was well-fed enough too.

My grandmother pulled a face, tutted and said, "Quite extraordinary," again.

I suppose I am quite extraordinary, but what happened that first evening at Barlington and in the days that followed makes my kind of extraordinary look not-very-extraordinary at all.

Do you hear what I hear?
If you hear an "ARGHHH!" then yes, you do

I was promptly packed off to bed and Mum followed, carrying Molly up to the nursery at the very top of the house. I am not keen on the name *nursery*, to be honest. It sounds a bit babyish, but it is basically a huge room with loads of beds where us kids always sleep. There were two other beds made up ready for Hugo and Fenella, who would be joining us the following night.

I wouldn't say I was excited, more intrigued about seeing my cousins again. It'd been a while since I'd seen them, and I had no idea what they were like now. I probably wouldn't have even recognized them if they'd come up and bitten me on the bum. All I could really remember about them was that they'd had bouncy blond curls and looked like they should be playing the harp and shooting love arrows.

Molly had woken up as soon as Mum put her into bed and was now having trouble getting back to sleep, what with her having slept the whole journey. Which meant I was also having trouble sleeping, what with Molly singing "Little Donkey" on repeat. She was very excited about performing in the family nativity. I think she wanted to make up for the school nativity where she played the wise man who brought gold. Mum had given her some Ferrero Rocher to act as the gift and she had eaten all thirty of them and thrown up all over one of the camel's hooves. She has no control when it comes to chocolate.

She was halfway through the eleventh-hundredth round of "Little Donkey" when we heard a *WHOOOOOSSHHH* noise, which sounded almost like a plane had flown dangerously close to the house. Both Molly and I bolted up in our beds.

She said, "What was that, Osky?"

But before I could answer, there was an almighty *WHOOOOOOOOOOOOMPH*. I was pretty sure something had landed on the roof. We both looked upwards and listened to whatever it was going *BUMP, BUMP, BUMP*.

This was followed by the sound of tiles falling off and smashing on the ground and then a bellowing noise which went a bit like this: *OOOHHHARGGHHHOO HOOOOHNOOOOOOOOOOOOOOOOO!*

That strange sound was then followed by the most brilliant flash of white light, which lit up the room through the gap in the curtains. Molly and I both gasped and shielded our eyeballs from the glare as the nursery was completely illuminated for a couple of seconds.

As soon as we were able to take our hands away from our faces, we ran over to the window and I threw back the curtains just in time to see *something* hurtling off the roof into the air. It careered across the sky like a very wibbly-wobbly meteor, making that *OOOGHHHOOHOOO HNOOOOOOOOOOOO!* noise again, and landed in the sheep field out the back of Barlington Hall with another almighty *WHOOOOOOOOOOOOMPH!*

The light it was emitting flickered and dimmed but didn't quite go out.

Molly turned to me, eyes as wide as saucers. "Was that Santa?"

"Santa? No, I don't think so," I said, but I was basing this purely on the fact it wasn't Christmas Eve and he usually comes equipped with presents and reindeer.

Molly grabbed my arm. "Is it the aliens from Kepler-452b coming back for Dad?"

"I don't know what it is," I said. "Maybe it's a light that's fallen off a passing plane or something?"

Molly frowned at me. "Lights don't make that *OOOOH OOOH AHHHH* noise, Osky."

I suppose she had a point, but I really hadn't the first idea what else it could be. I was actually beginning to think it *could* be the Keplorian-452-ers, but I didn't want to scare her with thoughts of an alien invasion. Although, to be honest, considering how things went, aliens may have turned out to be less trouble.

I opened the door to our bedroom and listened out for any sign that anyone else in the house had heard the strange noise, but all I could make out was the faint sound of snoring.

When I turned back round, Molly had her nose pushed right up against the window. "We should go and look. It could be something amazing! Some*one* amazing!"

She was clearly hoping for Santa. Whatever it was, it was still glowing slightly and would be easy enough to find. But I wasn't sure about traipsing off into a field in the middle of the night. It could be something amazing, but it could also be something dangerous, and that did scare me a little. And if Mum and Dad found out we'd snuck out after lights out, I knew *they'd* definitely be dangerous.

"I'm not sure, Molls. It's probably nothing," I said, very unconvincingly.

She grabbed me by the hand, flipped the hood of her Gruffalo onesie up and said, "That wasn't nothing, Oscar. Let's go see! We'll only be quick."

I looked back out at the light in the field. I kind of wanted to know what it was too.

"If you're scared, I'll protect you," Molly said.

Well, that left me zero choice. "I'm not scared and I'll be the one doing any protecting if it's required. But we'll have to go quick and you have to do what I say. We shouldn't really be heading out alone."

"I know! But it could be Santa!" Molly jumped up and down a couple of times so her furry hood bobbled about, and then she squealed, "This. Is. So. Exciting!"

I slipped on a hoodie and we both took our welly boots – my green ones and Molly's gold sparkly ones – to put on when we got to the back door. I picked up our scarves, which we'd left in a heap on the floor, and wrapped Molly's around her neck. I also picked up what looked like an antique cricket bat from the toy box – just in case.

We crept down the first flight of stairs and tiptoed past the bedroom where Mum and Dad were snoring in unison, then down another set of stairs, along the corridors and through a wing of the house that isn't used much, until we found the back door.

I noticed a torch hanging from one of the coat hooks by the door. "I'll have that," I said and grabbed it. I handed Molly the cricket bat, which wasn't the best idea as it turned out. Then carefully I turned the key in the lock and nudged the door open. It made a really big creaking noise, but luckily Barlington is so big I knew no one would have heard it.

"Quickly, to the fence." I stepped outside, my breath making a white cloud in front of me.

"Do you think it's cold enough to snow?" Molly asked. "I really want a snowy white Christmas."

"Nah, it never really snows at Christmastime, not in England anyway," I said. "Now, come on, let's see what it is and get back inside quickly."

"I think it will definitely-wefinitely snow!" Molly said and then she raced across the back lawn, swinging the bat like a helicopter blade above her head. It wasn't exactly what I'd call professional-standard creeping, but luckily there was nobody about to notice. I ran after her and helped her unsnag herself from the barbed wire that ran between the fence posts, separating the sheep field from the garden.

When we were both over the fence, I flicked on the torch to light the way and so we could avoid any massive sheep poos. We ran towards the end of the field, where we could still make out the faint glow of whatever it was that had bounced off the roof. It was a chilly December night, and the torchlight made our breath look like little clouds.

When we were about thirty metres away, I slowed down and grabbed Molly's hand to pull her back before she got too close, and turned off the torch so whatever or whoever it was couldn't see us approaching.

"What is it?" Molly whispered again, in a voice that

really wasn't a whisper.

I squinted. It was hard to tell. From where I was standing it looked like a bundle of white material. A bundle of lightly glowing white material.

"It looks like somebody's washing," I said.

"Washing doesn't cry, Osky."

"Cry?"

I strained to hear and Molly was right. I *could* hear sobbing.

Slowly, I walked forward, Molly creeping along beside me. As we got closer, I could see whatever it was moving slightly – shaking, even.

I stopped a few metres away and managed to find my voice to say, "Hey, are you alright?"

I must have startled it, because it leaped upwards and made a sound a bit like this:

"AGGHHHHHHHHHHHHHHGAHGAHGAHGAHGAH GAHGARFFFF!"

Which made me make a sound a bit like this: *"WAAAAAAAAAAARGGHHHH!"* (Because I was startled too and not because I was scared.)

And Molly made a sound a bit like this: *"WA WA WOO WA!"* which was a much happier and more amazed sound than either of the previous two. And then she put her hand on mine and said, "Don't worry, Osky, it's only an angel!"

5

Oh, holy night! The stars are brightly shining...

unless...hang on, that's not a star!

So there we were, standing in a sheep field in the middle of night with what Molly thought was an angel.

"It's not an angel, Molly," I said, spectacularly incorrectly. "It's just a man dressed in a sheet, with a halo hovering above his head...somehow." I shone my torch at him. "You okay? How did you end up in the field?"

Molly said, "He's an angel, Osky, he probably flew here."

The just-a-man-in-a-sheet sprang back and held out one hand in Molly's direction. "Stay back, beast! What are you, oh furry being that speaks?"

"She's not a beast," I said.

He shrieked, "But she looks like a beast! A beast which stands upon its hind legs! Stay back, I command you!"

Molly giggled and waved her cricket bat. "I'm not a beastie, I'm Molly, silly!"

The man actually cowered. "Please do not strike me, furry one, I am a celestial being and I have powers which you cannot comprehend. Granted, I don't have them this very moment, but they will return, of that I am certain!"

"You speak funny, celestial bean!" Molly said and waggled the bat at him again.

And he shrieked. Again.

"Have mercy, foul creature," he said, still holding up a hand as though it would protect him.

I took the cricket bat from Molly's hand, hoping it might help him calm down.

"She's not a foul creature or a beast or a furry one! She's a five-year-old girl and she's not going to strike you. Molly, take your hood down, show him."

Molly flopped her hood down and did a massive grin.

"See, it's only a Gruffalo onesie."

The bloke covered his face with his hands. "I cannot

cast mine eyes on such abominable wretchedness! A child swallowed up by a *Gruffalo*? I have never heard of such horrors. Or a Gruffalo, for that matter. Lord, it is apparent that I am condemned to walk in the land of the doomed!"

The guy seemed a little over the top to me, but at that point I still hadn't figured out that he was an actual angel. Sure, the halo was a big clue, but when you've made up your mind that something isn't real, it's easy to dismiss the evidence even when it's shining in your eyeballs.

"Gruffalos don't really exist! It's just a costume! You know, like the get-up you're wearing. I think you need to calm down," I said. "This is Chipping Bottom. It's quite a nice little village, actually. Nobody around here is doomed."

"If I do not reverse the mistake that I have made, then we are all doomed! Dooooomed, I say!"

"Do you think you might have hit your head?" I asked. "I once dived right into the goalpost while I was making a spectacular save and I went a bit funny after that. Concussion, the school nurse reckoned. I can see if we can call the village doctor. I'm sure Chipping Bottom has one."

"Chipping Bottom?" He tilted his head. "Where is that? Where in Heaven's name am I?"

"Sheepies field. Near Barlington Hall. Chipping Bottom. Hampshire. England. The British Isles. The United Kingdom. The world," Molly said quite triumphantly.

"The Isles of the Sea?" he said and sort of crumpled down onto the floor, his sheet bunching around him like a nest. "I am a long way from Bethlehem."

"Granny Roberts used to live there," Molly said. "It is loads of hours in Colin from here. That's why we travel at night."

"She lived in Birmingham, Molls, not Bethlehem," I corrected. I shone my torch at the man's face and noticed he had very nice skin – luminous, even. "Are you sure you didn't take a blow to the head? You are acting very... *strangely.*"

He looked at me with frantic eyes. "What time is it?"

"Late, after midnight." I looked over towards Barlington and started thinking about all the times Mum and Dad told us not to go wandering off without a grown-up. This was probably why – you don't know what sort of trouble you're going to go wandering yourself into.

We needed to head back.

"No!" The man clutched his hands together. "I mean what century?"

Odd question. "The twenty-first," I said slowly.

That didn't go down well. "The twenty-first? This cannot be! I have travelled forward in time two thousand years Anno Domini!"

Molly scrunched up her nose. "Anno Dom and I?"

"He means after the birth of Jesus," I said.

His hand shot to his face. "But there has been no birth! God forgive me. It's all ruined! Ruined, I tell you! I only wanted to do justice to my first major announcing – you know, inject a little extra power?"

"No, I do not know," Molly said, quite brightly and clearly not reading the atmosphere.

He started crying again – well, more wailing really – and I started to feel a bit awkward and even more anxious that we'd snuck out. I decided that we should probably just leave him to do his crying and wailing on his own.

"Whatever it is that's happened, I'm sure it's not as bad as you think. Things will seem better in the morning," I said, because that's what Mum says to me whenever I have a problem. And sometimes she's right. "So...we

61

might just be getting back...okay? Maybe you should think about heading home too?"

I jerked my head towards the house so Molly would get the picture.

"Home? I cannot get home. Things will not seem better in the morning, for what I have done will cause unimaginable damage!"

"It was only a few roof tiles," I said.

He threw his arms wide. "Through my very actions I may have inadvertently brought about the most terrible change to history as we know it. Somewhere, close to this Sheepies Field, near Barlington Hall, Chipping Bottom, Hampshire, England, the British Isles, the United Kingdom, the world, roameth the Virgin Mary, carrying the baby child Jesus Christ within her. So too doth her husband Joseph, and Balthazar the wise man and a shepherd and quite possibly a donkey, all walking upon this strange soil."

For a moment, I did not know what to say to all of that. I looked at Molly and she just giggled. I bent down so I was on the same level as him. "Are you one hundred per cent certain you didn't get bopped on the head?" I decided to try asking him the same questions the school nurse asked me. "Can you tell me your name? Maybe your address?"

"My name is Gabriel and I come from the Kingdom of Glory."

Clearly, he was a few sheepies short of a flock. "I'm going to go and call you a doctor. I think you're a bit... confused."

Molly bent down next to me and screwed up her face like she was really examining him closely. Then she did a big smile and said, "Nice to meet you, Angel Gabriel." Then she elbowed me and said, "See, I told you he was an angel."

"I'm not just *an* angel. I'm *Archangel* Gabriel!"

"Oh yeah! You're the biggest, most importantest one, aren't you? Mrs Okoye said that Christians believe you appeared unto Mary and told her God was going to put a baby in her tummy," Molly said.

"She is quite right, on all counts, but who is Mrs Okoye?" the Angel Gabriel asked.

"She's my teacher. When I go back to school she's going to be very excited that I met the Angel Gabriel!"

I splutter-laughed at that. "He's clearly a bit confused! He's probably got lost on the way home from a nativity

63

play or a Christmas party or something. He's *so* not the Angel Gabriel, Molls!"

And then the Angel Gabriel rose to his feet and extended two giant, other-worldly wings behind him, which engulfed him in a glowing, swirling mist of silvery-white. It was magnificent and shocking and completely unbelievable.

Then he said, "But I am he."

6

Angels from the Realms of...
Chipping Bottom?

Neither Molly nor I said anything for several moments. We just stood there with our mouths down to our ankles and our eyes blasted open in total surprise.

Eventually, I managed to speak. Well, actually I said, "I...I...I...pffffff," and then I stopped and stared some more.

"Don't worry, take your time," Angel Gabriel said. "I'm used to this sort of response. Such impressive majesty can take you mortals by surprise."

I had to admit it, he did look pretty impressive. Radiantly magnificent even. If he wasn't an angel, he was doing a very good impression of one.

Molly tugged on my sleeve. "Osky," she whispered in a very un-whisperly way again. "I think that he might actually be the actual Angel Gabriel."

"Errr...maybe...no...he can't be. It's not possible." My voice was more breath than sound.

"But he has the big flappy wings," she said.

"Yeah, I had noticed those."

"And the spangly halo."

"Yup, spotted that too."

"And his skin is really, really, *really* smooth."

The Angel Gabriel smiled. "Thank you. It isn't a prerequisite but all angels do seem to have a flawless complexion."

"Just like a baby's bum," Molly said.

"Why thank— what? No, not like a baby's bum at all!"

"He also went BOOM from the sky in a really, really, *really* bright light," Molly continued. "And I know he was doing all that wailing and being all doomy, but I think he is actually quite...*heavenly*."

I was getting a vibe from him too...maybe it *was* heavenly.

Eventually I said, "So we're thinking he is probably

the Angel Gabriel?" It sounded so unlikely, so improbable, but looking at him standing there being so completely angel-y, I couldn't think of any other explanation as to who or what he could be.

Molly nodded. "Yup, probably. Hello, the Angel Gabriel!" Then she said, "Are you going to go back up to Heaven to be with Harold?"

The Probably Angel Gabriel looked confused. "You call God *Harold*?"

Molly fell about laughing.

"Harold's her goldfish," I explained. "Her dead goldfish."

The Probably Angel Gabriel looked Molly up and down and said, "How unexpected."

Which was a bit rich coming from an angel in a sheep field.

"It's okay. He's happy now, swimming about in fishy Heaven." Molly opened and closed her mouth in a gulpy way and flip-flapped her hands like little fins.

The Probably Angel Gabriel pulled a face. "What *is* she doing?"

"Pretending to be a heavenly goldfish. Look, are you here on a mission?" I said, getting the conversation back on track. "What were you talking about before when you mentioned Mary and Joseph?"

The Angel Gabriel blushed and his wings folded down. "I seem to be stuck here."

"You should use your angel-y powers and fly yourself home," Molly said, flapping her arms up and down.

"I've tried that, but, alas, my powers seem not to be working here."

"Did you try properly, like, really try your bestest?" Molly asked.

"Yes," he said, "watch."

The angel spread his arms out wide, then raised them above his head and looked up at the inky black night sky. I took a step back and pulled Molly closer to me, because who knew what might happen? The Angel Gabriel pulled a strained face – he looked like he was holding his breath and really concentrating. His halo flickered even brighter and he grew redder and redder and I began to wonder if he might be in danger of exploding or something. But then his halo dimmed a bit and he did this massive exhale and said, "See, nothing. I'm well and truly stuck here. And I very much need to not be stuck here."

"What are you going to do?" Molly asked.

"Well, I have an idea, but I might need your help in order to return from where and whence I came. I believe my powers will be restored when I have found all those who do not belong here."

"Our help?" I said, very confused. "To get your powers back?"

"Okay!" Molly said. Which is *so* Molly to volunteer for something before she even knows what she's actually agreeing to.

"Hang on a minute," I said, trying to be the sensible one, "what are you asking us to do, exactly? I don't know anything about angel power."

"You want me to go over it *again*?"

"I'm sorry," I said, politely but firmly, "it's just that I might need a bit more time and possibly a few more teeny details to get my head around the fact that I'm talking to an angel. An angel who wants our help."

"Why must human brains always be so primitive?" he said, I think more to himself than anyone else. "I require your assistance in navigating this strange land and time. You will help me locate the holy party – Mary, Joseph, the wise man, the shepherd – and get them all back to

Bethlehem so Jesus, the Son of God, can be born where and *when* he is supposed to be born and the world can be how *the Lord* planned it to be. We must find them all, and only then, when I have them all gathered around me, will I be able to use my powers and return to Bethlehem."

"Right...and if we don't?"

"The birth of the baby Jesus is to be a much-celebrated occasion – if it does not come to pass as *He* wishes, there will be dire consequences for humankind." He said that last bit *very* dramatically and swooshed his arms about a bit.

"Sounds a bit gloomy. But what's in it for *us* exactly? Why should we get involved?" I asked.

His jaw dropped to his bare feet. "In it for *you*? Other than the birth of Jesus Christ not coming to pass as it should and the cataclysmic effect that will have?"

I pondered things for a moment and a terrible thought struck me. "Hang on – are you saying that there will be no *Christmas*?"

Molly gasped and covered her ears as though she couldn't bear to even hear it.

The Angel Gabriel nodded gravely. "And more importantly, no baby king born in a stable in Bethlehem."

"Yeah, but NO CHRISTMAS! That can't happen! What about all the presents?"

He sighed. "Slightly misplaced priorities, but yes, there will be no presents."

"Hang on...how do you know all this? You come from the past, you don't even have Christmas yet!"

"I am an angel, I come from no time. I am eternal. And eternal beings have a mysterious way of knowing things. An innate understanding of the world, shall we say."

"Well, what I'm understanding is there'll be no carolling, no putting out stockings for Santa or a carrot for Rudolph!" I stopped and gasped for a breath as the enormity of what NO CHRISTMAS actually meant hit me.

Molly squealed. "Poor Rudolph, he'll starve!"

"No Christmas dinner, no baking Christmas cookies with Mum, no watching family Christmas movies and no roasting chestnuts by an open fire?" I don't know why I said that last one, we've never done that.

"Santa's elves, Osky!" Molly gasped, then looked at me with huge, concerned eyes. "They'll lose their jobs!"

A thought more dreadful than unemployed elves then walloped me in the brain lobes. "OH, DOUBLE HANG ON!

If there's no Christmas, then there will be NO ME!"

The Angel Gabriel frowned. "I'm afraid I don't follow."

"My parents met on Christmas Day when Dad was singing carols. So if there is no Christmas Day, they won't meet and if they don't meet, they won't get married and have ME! Or Molly, but mainly no ME!"

The Angel Gabriel looked a little confused but did not deny that what I was saying was true. Instead, he said, "Yes...*no you* is a...possibility, and that is why we must make haste and find the Holy Mother Mary and Joseph and those others at once!"

I was all of a tizzy-flutter. "I'll run back and get on the phone to the emergency services and get them to send out a search party!" I said and grabbed Molly's elbow, ready to make a dash for it.

But the Angel Gabriel held up a commanding hand. "No, I'm afraid you won't be doing that."

"Why not? This is a Christmas emergency!"

"Well, for starters, people will not believe you."

"I'll make them believe me. I know! You can get your big flappity wings out again and flash your halo, that'll convince them!"

73

"An impossibility, I'm afraid. There are strict rules and quotas."

"Rules and quotas? I mean, *whaaaaaaaaaattttt*?"

"Yes, yes," he said impatiently. "An angel can only appear to *special* humans when commanded to do so by the Lord God Himself."

"But you appeared to us!"

"Like a big ball of wailing washing," Molly said.

"Normally I would never allow mere mortals to cast their eyes on me, but I was in a place of great woe and confusion. I absolutely cannot let any more humans see me. The consequences are too dire to mention. No, with regards to assistance, I'm afraid I am stuck with you two."

"I have my own lightsaber," Molly said proudly, which confused both me and the Angel Gabriel. Honestly, sometimes I do not know what goes on in her head.

"So what happens if the system breaks down?" I asked.

"My angeling licence will be revoked."

"What does that mean?" Molly asked.

"That I would just be Gabriel. All angeling privileges would be over."

"Well, that doesn't sound too bad," I said brightly.

"And I might be cast out of Heaven for all eternity."

"Okay...that would be a shame, but, again, I'm only hearing of problems for you. I really think we should get some more help on board."

"And also the world as you know it may end... *possibly*."

"Oh, you're kidding! What do you mean, *possibly*?"

"Angels remain in Heaven, humans on Earth and never the two shall meet, unless God decides it's a good idea. That is how it is and that is how it must be or the entire system will break down. The power of Heaven is that it runs on faith not fact. It's hard to know the *exact* impact of somebody seeing me who shouldn't, but do you want to take that risk? We're already in a bit of a muddle. It's probably a good idea not to make things any worse."

"A bit of a muddle! My very existence is being threatened," I said. "If we don't find Mary, Joseph, a wise man, a shepherd – and did you say a *donkey*? – that you have accidentally littered across the countryside, Christmas is doomed. And you're now telling me if we get any help or tell anybody, we are also doomed."

"DOOM, DOOM, DOOOOOOMED!" Molly said, stomping about in her wellies like she was having a lovely time. "DOUBLE DOOMEDY-DOOOOOMED!"

"Exactly! She's got it!" the Angel Gabriel said, with a smile that didn't seem appropriate in the circumstances. "Now, let us go, at once!"

He swung around and started marching purposefully across the field.

I didn't know what to do. Things seemed pretty amazingly terrible, but I didn't think I could just trot off on some quest at that precise moment. It required some thought, some planning and clothes suitable for the cold winter weather. I shivered and pulled my scarf tighter round my neck. The sky was cloudless and the air had a frosty bite to it.

"Hey," I shouted after him, "we can't go looking for historical people now! It's the middle of the night! We're only wearing our jim-jams! And it's dark. Besides, our parents will worry if we go missing!"

"And now I am only really hearing problems for you," the Angel Gabriel shouted back. "Come now, it is time for you to find Mary and the others and save Christmas."

"Hang on a mistletoeing-minute!" A thought struck

me. "Can't you give God a call? He should be able to sort this mess out, no? He is the Almighty, after all. Just give him a holler!"

The Angel Gabriel stopped suddenly, then turned around very slowly. "Ah, yes. About Him. I just think it's best if He doesn't know about this situation. I'd really rather you didn't mention it to Him. In fact, let's keep all this to ourselves. And one does not give God a *holler*."

"But I thought God knows everything!" I said.

"I believe He does, but He also works in mysterious ways. This is probably all part of His plan. Probably. If this is a test, we just need to get on with it. If He wants to help, He will, but it is important for people and angels to help themselves too."

"Yeah but—"

"Also, I want to give Him a bit of a break."

"Like a holibobs?" Molly said.

"Not *exactly*. It's just He's had a very busy time of it. What with actually making the world and then sending plagues and locusts and floods – that sort of thing takes it out of you. Do you know how many prayers are said every single day?"

I shrugged.

"Well, the answer is *a lot*. He has a lot to think about, especially with the baby coming. I refuse to add to His workload. So, onwards!"

He swished his gown and started across the field again.

"But you need to call Him! This is serious!"

The Angel Gabriel stopped in his tracks again. "No! He trusted me! He gave me two instructions when I got the job. Number one: don't forget to feed the cats—" He frowned. "No, hang on, that's not right. That was Angel Ariel – she's in charge of animals. God said: 'Number one, Gabriel, you shall be the strong one, and number two, you shall be the divine messenger', which, reading between the lines, meant *Do not mess up the baby-announcing thing*. I will not let Him down. We need to do this my way, or...or...or I SHALL SMITE YOU AND YOUR HOUSE!"

He said that in a very boomy voice and raised both his hands like he actually meant to smite us. I am not completely sure what that is – *smiting* – but I guessed it wouldn't be lovely. But the smiting didn't happen. He lowered his hands and looked at them in disappointment.

"Blast it! Forgot I had no powers for a moment there."

"Did you just try and smite us?" I said.

"Nope."

"Hmmmm, I think you did. Look, if it really is down to us to save Christmas and—"

"Stop all the DOOOOOM!" Molly interrupted.

"Yes, stop all the doom, we promise to help. But it will have to be tomorrow. We'll come back and help you search as soon as we can."

To be honest, I was secretly hoping that if we went back to sleep, we might wake up to find this had all been a really weird and horrifying nightmare.

The Angel Gabriel did a very dramatic sigh and said, "Fine, tomorrow it is." Then he sat down on the ground.

"What are you doing now?" I asked, a bit impatiently.

"Waiting for tomorrow."

I did my own big dramatic sigh. "You can't sit in a field all night. It's freezing. Come on, you can come back with us, but you'll have to keep quiet and stay hidden. We can start Operation Save Christmas tomorrow."

He stood back up. "Yes, that is more agreeable. And I like the sound of Operation Save Christmas, it sounds quite positive."

"You're welcome," I said and started leading the way back. "And maybe you could turn that thing off?" I pointed to his halo. "It's a bit bright, someone's going to notice."

He gasped loudly. "You're right! But I can't turn it off!"

"We're going to have to do something about that then."

We snuck in through the back door, took our wellies off and crept along the corridor, trying to find somewhere for the Angel Gabriel to hide for the night. The whole time I was whispering to myself, "I've got an angel in the house, I've got an angel in the house, totally normal, don't panic."

Eventually, we settled on a downstairs bathroom in the part of the house which is no longer used. You might think a bathroom would be pretty small, but this one is huge.

"Enough room to do two roly-polys," Molly said, and then demonstrated.

The Angel Gabriel looked around. "A throne, how

wonderful!" Then he closed the toilet seat lid, sat himself down and made himself comfortable.

I gave Molly the job of finding something to put over his halo, because, even with the bathroom door closed, light spilled out under the gap at the bottom.

She came back with a tea cosy.

Possibly not my first choice, but it would do.

"Put this on your head," I said, taking it from Molly and handing it to the Angel Gabriel.

He wrinkled up his nose like he didn't really want to, but I gave him my best glare and he put it on and squashed his halo down.

Molly did a yawn so big I could almost see her perfectly healthy tonsils. I checked my watch. "Right, the Angel Gabriel, it's almost two in the morning and we need to get some sleep. You stay here until we come and get you, understand?"

He nodded. "I must say, I do rather like all this *the* Angel Gabriel. The '*the*' makes me sound very important. Like I'm the *most* important angel."

"Are there other angels?" I asked.

"There's the archangel Michael, he's in charge of all the angels. And there are loads of others that don't really have names. There's one who threw a giant boulder into the sea, and one who ensures that people behave and if they don't he has them eaten by worms—"

"They don't sound very heavenly," I said.

"I ate a worm once," Molly said, which was unfortunately true. I was there to witness the moment in its full horror.

"I've only heard of the one who announces stuff," I said.

"That's ME! I'm the one who announces stuff! Ha! I knew announcing was an important undertaking. For it is *I*, not the angel of the worms or the angel of the boulder, who is remembered by name by those who walk on God's Earth! Yes, there is much dignity in announcing!"

"I'm happy for you," I said. "We'd better go, we'll need some sleep before we start our quest to find Mary and Joseph and that shepherd and the wise man and possibly a donkey tomorrow. Now stay here and don't move."

"Goodnight." The Angel Gabriel nodded at us as if we were dismissed and Molly and I crept back up to our room, leaving him sitting on his toilet throne with a tea cosy on his head.

There wasn't long until morning and I needed to sleep, but as soon as my head hit the pillow, my brain started buzzing. Christmas and my very existence were under threat. Tomorrow would be the twenty-first of December, which meant I only had four full days to sort it all out before midnight on Christmas Eve. I mean, I definitely thought I was worth saving, but I couldn't stop thinking about what it would be like with no Christmas. Christmas means so much to so many people. I've always felt it's a magical time of year. That feeling of excitement you get when you count down the days. Hanging out the stockings on Christmas Eve. Having to lie in bed because you've woken up too early and your parents won't let you down to see the tree until at least seven o'clock. Opening your presents and the look on people's faces when you see them open theirs. It is joyous and special and it brings people together.

And while I lay there, with festive thoughts and worries about a lost wise man and a far-wandering shepherd, something else came into my mind. My grandfather.

As far as I knew, angels were pretty powerful beings. I began to wonder... If I did Gabriel a favour, then maybe, once he had his powers back, he might do me one in return.

Little Donkey, Little Donkey,

peeing in the pond

The following morning, I was woken by the loud clanging of the bell for breakfast. I had that thing, you know, when you wake up and you can't work out where you are because you're sleeping somewhere new? And then I had that thing where I couldn't remember if I really had met the Angel Gabriel in a sheep field and whether I actually was now responsible for making sure the baby Jesus was born in Bethlehem two-thousand-and-odd years earlier and helping save Christmas and life as we know it.

Thinking about it, that second thing is probably not actually a *thing* for many people. I sat up, ready to ask

Molly if it had all actually happened or if I'd just done some very powerful dreaming, but she wasn't in her bed. Her Gruffalo onesie was lying at the foot of it though, looking a bit damp, so I figured that she had probably had a wee-whoopsie and already been retrieved from the room by Mum or Dad.

I changed and hurried down the stairs, heading towards the bathroom on the other side of the house, to check whether there really was an angel in there. By the time I got to the door, I'd pretty much convinced myself it had all been a dream and put it down to my impressively active imagination.

But when I went inside, there, sitting on the closed toilet lid with his tea cosy still on his head, was the Angel Gabriel, exactly as we had left him.

"Right. You do really exist then."

"Yes, of course I exist and I am glorious!" the angel proclaimed and got to his feet.

Glorious and a bit of a big-head, frankly.

He clasped his hands together and looked at me earnestly. "I understand all the awe and wonder. I am, after all, awe-inspiring and wondrous by nature, but we really must depart, there is much work to do."

"I can't go just yet."

He tilted his head and his tea cosy slipped over one eye. "And why not?"

"I haven't had my breakfast. I can't go on a quest for Mary and Joseph on an empty stomach. Besides, I can't just disappear, my parents will ask questions. I'll have to talk them into letting me go out. Molly and I will come and find you as soon as I've sorted things. Just stay here and don't move. Won't be long."

He did another sigh, bigger this time, and sat back down on the loo. "Right, fine, that's okay. The world as we know it hangs in the balance, today is already the twenty-first of December, but you go off and feast, like you mortals must."

"A bowl of Frosted Flakes is hardly a feast. I'll be back soon, promise! Then we'll crack on with Operation Save Christmas and go find Mary and Joseph, that wise man, the shepherd and you said possibly a donkey, right?"

"Yes, possibly a donkey."

I paused, then said, "Wow, you really messed up, didn't you?"

"An unfortunate accident, which I aim to fix, once

somebody has had their all-important Frosted Flakes – whatever they might be!"

I ignored that little cereal-based dig and darted back down the corridor towards the dining room, telling myself that everything would be fine.

I passed by the library, which was filled to the ceiling with old books and where my grandparents keep their ancient-looking computer. Then I went by another sitting room and a room which looked like it was used solely for displaying photographs of old pets. I finally arrived at the dining room.

Someone had gone to a lot of trouble setting the table to make it all Christmassy. There was a deep red tablecloth on it and the napkins had little robins on holly sprigs embroidered into them. We don't even go to that much trouble on Christmas Day!

"Nice flowers," I said, nodding at the centrepiece.

"Poinsettias," Grandfather replied. "Cheery, aren't they?"

"Hey, champ!" Dad said. "Come and wrap your face around some of this food."

My grandmother raised her eyebrows from behind her copy of *The Telegraph* and said, "Good morning,

Oscar. I trust you slept well."

I hadn't, but somehow I didn't think telling her the truth about our late-night trip outside to find the Angel Gabriel would be that believable. Grown-ups are very short-sighted about that sort of thing.

"Fancy a kipper?" Grandfather said and waggled a fork with a yellow fish stuck on its prongs at me. "Margaret's outdone herself with this spread."

Margaret is the housekeeper at Barlington Hall, and Grandfather was right, she'd gone to town with breakfast. But I'm more of a cereal-in-the-morning person than a smoked-fish-in-the-morning person, so I sat down, trying to appear normal, and said, "No, you're alright."

"No, thank you," Dad corrected.

"Morning, Osky!" Molly shouted in my face when I sat down opposite her. She was trying to cut the top off her boiled egg, but she wasn't having much luck because of the sparkly mittens she was wearing with her unicorn costume. So then she started bashing the egg, which made Grandmother tut from behind her newspaper.

"Your sister here has been regaling us with fanciful stories about angels!" Grandfather said.

"What?!" I shouted, a bit too loudly.

"The shiny one that looked like laundry!"

I glared at Molly – she really has no control over that motormouth of hers. Molly did not pick up on the glare though and just did this humungous grin back at me. I made a note to have words with her later about not shouting her mouth off.

"She's got a big imagination, that's all," I said, hoping that I had chosen a tone which did not give away the fact that I had an angel stashed in the loo.

Grandmother said, "So it would seem," so I think I chose an excellently convincing tone. Well done me.

Mum bowled into the room, looking a bit bedraggled, with her hair sticking up in all different directions and still wearing her Scrooge nightie that Dad got her last Christmas. It said, Bah, Humbug!

"Cathy, how nice that you feel so relaxed as to arrive at the breakfast table in your night-time garments. Although I would describe that attire as anything but jolly."

Mum said, "Good morning, Araminta," like it wasn't really a good morning, and plopped herself down next to me. She ruffled my hair, which she knows I find annoying but she still does it anyway. Then she said, "Posture, Oscar. You're sitting like a prawn," which she knows also irritates me. I mean, would you enjoy being likened to a crustacean? Exactly. Although, not my biggest problem right then.

Grandmother folded up her paper and placed it on the table. "Did you enjoy your lie-in? I must say, it must be lovely to languish in bed with nothing to do."

"It's eight in the morning, I'd hardly call that a lie-in," Mum said, chasing a poached egg around a silver plate with a serving spoon.

"No, I imagine you wouldn't. But hopefully all that extra rest has made you energized for our first rehearsal of the nativity this afternoon. This year is an extra-special year and particularly important to Reginald." Grandmother glanced over at Grandfather. "It marks the one hundredth year that the Cuthbert-Andersons have been performing at St Bartholomew's. I am certain you will all be thrilled when you hear what I have planned. It *will* be special. And all the proceeds from the donation basket will go to the funding of the new church roof! We must do our bit for the community, now, mustn't we?"

Bottoms! I'd forgotten that we'd actually be needed for rehearsals. How was I supposed to do something heroic like save Christmas and life as we knew it when I was prancing around in a fake beard acting shepherdy?

Margaret the housekeeper came into the room to clear the plates. She had an excited look in her eyes and was hovering around near Grandmother like she really wanted to say something. A worrying thought immediately worried me – what if she'd stumbled across my messenger from the Lord hiding in the lavatory?

"What is it, Margaret?" Grandmother said. "You're hovering around me like a house fly in a cardigan."

"You'll never guess what, Lady Cuthbert-Anderson!" Margaret said. "The strangest thing has happened!"

My danger-senses pricked up, causing me to choke and make a Frostie shoot out of my nose. If Margaret was about to say that she'd found an angel in the downstairs loo, there'd be nothing for it, I'd have to rugby-tackle her to the floor. It probably would be frowned upon if I launched myself at her and wrestled her out the room, but Christmas and possibly my life depended on it, so I'd do it if I had to.

"Everyone on the village WhatsApp has been talking about it."

Go carefully, Margaret, I thought. *This boy is ready to wrestle.*

"I am not on the village WhatsApp," Grandmother said curtly.

"There were strange sightings in the village last night. Apparently something dropped out of the sky and made a hole clean through the roof of George Budwell's barn."

It took me a moment to assess the information. Initially, when I heard "dropped out of the sky", I got ready to lead with the shoulder and go in low by her ankles...but then I realized she couldn't be talking about the Angel Gabriel – he'd ricocheted off our roof, not a barn.

Close call, Margaret. But in that case, who had dropped into George Budwell's?

"He saw a bright flash of light," she continued, "heard a loud bang and noticed the damage from his upstairs window."

"Our angel came in a flash of flight, like this – KABOOOM!" Molly said and threw her arms in the air, but luckily everybody ignored her.

"Goodness, was anyone hurt, Margaret?" Grandfather said.

"Not that I've heard. George raced to find out what the commotion was and saw a man take off into the fields. He was very well-dressed apparently, in a fancy cloak, some sort of hat and carrying something under his arm. George said he would have chased after him, if he had been wearing more than just his underpants and slippers."

"Do you think it was a burglar?" Mum asked.

"A well-dressed burglar, burgling a barn? Doubt it!" Dad laughed. "What was he after, a couple of hay bales?"

Mum did not laugh. Instead, she scowled at Dad. "He could have been after some expensive farming equipment."

"Possibly, Cathy. But it doesn't sound quite right to me. Perhaps someone messing about. Most likely a townie staying in one of the hotels," Grandfather said.

It didn't sound like a burglar to me, but it also didn't sound like a townie either.

It sounded like a missing wise man. Which was brilliant news and the reason why I accidentally shouted out, "Brilliant!"

"Brilliant?" Mum said. "What do you mean?"

"I just mean everything is all very...brilliant. I'm just so pleased to be here, you know, us all together, doing the nativity."

"Ah yes, back to that," Grandmother said, then looked at Margaret accusingly. "The breakfast table really is not the place for idle village gossip."

Grandfather gave Grandmother a wink. "Because no one here enjoys listening to gossip, do they, Minty, darling?"

A small smile flickered across Grandmother's lips. "Nor is it the place for teasing, Reginald." Then she turned to Margaret and said, "Thank you, that will be all."

Margaret disappeared off to the kitchen, arms stacked high with dirty dishes. When she was gone, Grandmother said, "And so to the nativity. My plan is to go through your parts after lunch when the others have arrived..." She suddenly trailed off, as though something had distracted her. She rose to her feet, a look of pure horror on her face. "Good grief, is that a—"

"AN EEEE-AWWWW!" Molly shouted before she could finish.

Grandmother clutched her hand to her chest. "I think she's right! Reginald! Is that a donkey in the rose garden?"

Mum, Dad and I swung round so we could see, and

Grandfather swapped the glasses that were on his face for the ones which were hanging around his neck. "Yes, Minty, darling. That is indeed a donkey in the rose garden."

"Brilliant!" I shouted again, which got a few looks.

But it *was* brilliant – the "possibly a donkey" that the Angel Gabriel had mentioned he might have catapulted from the past was in fact a "definitely a donkey" and it was in the garden!

What a breakfast! Biblical beings were popping up all over the place!

Which was great in respect to collecting them all up to save Crimbo, but slightly problematic in that my family might put it all together and figure out that Mary, Joseph, a shepherd and a wise man were on the loose in Chipping Bottom. And as we had to solve this problem discreetly so as not to mess up the entire planet, I immediately knew that no one could know that the donkey was special...so I panicked and shouted, "No! Not brilliant! That is NOT a donkey!"

Everyone looked at me strangely. Probably firstly because of the *Brilliant! No, not brilliant* outburst and secondly because it was very obviously a donkey.

Looking back, I think the events of the previous night coupled with the ones at breakfast might have all got a bit too much for me at this point.

"Well, it's not a rhinoceros, Oscar!" Dad said, correctly but I think quite unsupportively.

"It's an EEEE-AWWW!" Molly shouted again. Then she got off her chair and started doing donkey kicks across the dining room floor.

"It could be a horse?" I said, but even I knew I didn't

sound convincing. Then the donkey quickly put a stop to my already incredibly weak argument that it wasn't a donkey, by doing a very loud *"EEE-AWWW!"* which made the windowpanes rattle.

"Yeah, that's a donkey," I admitted.

"How did a donkey get into the rose garden?" Grandmother asked. "And a very mangy-looking donkey at that!"

"Perhaps it has escaped from Lady Asster's donkey sanctuary?" Grandfather suggested. "It's just over the back fields, near to George Budwell's place in fact."

"Yes, that's most probably it," Grandmother said.

It is possible that I had worried unnecessarily in thinking that on spotting our back-garden visitor, my family would make the leap to it being Mary and Joseph's donkey which the Angel Gabriel had accidentally transported in the middle of its journey from Nazareth.

"What's it doing out there?" Mum said.

Dad tilted his head. "It would appear to be emptying its bladder."

He was right. We all watched in stunned silence as the donkey backed itself up over the ornamental fish pond and started to fill it up.

"WOW-WEEEEE!" Molly laughed.

If you've never seen a donkey take a piddle, I can tell you, it is quite impressive. Although I couldn't imagine it going down well with Grandmother.

But she seemed surprisingly delighted. "Oh, Reginald, this is a sign!"

"A sign?" everybody echoed, because I think we were all a bit confused. Signs are things like massive stars in the sky in the East, not a donkey doing an enormo wee.

Grandmother clapped her hands together. "Yes! I do believe I've just had the most wonderful of ideas."

I began to worry about where Grandmother was going with this for two reasons. Number one: she wasn't allowed to have ideas for that particular donkey when he had the important job of delivering the Holy Mother to Bethlehem. And number two: what wonderful idea could ever spring forth from a piddling donkey?

Which is why everybody looked very confused and said, "You have?" at the exact same time.

"This donkey has strayed here for a reason."

"It has?" everybody said in unison again.

"Yes! Wouldn't it be wonderful to have a real-life donkey in our nativity? Far better than Morris, that ill-

100

behaved sheep. It would surely show the likes of Mrs Tadworth that the Cuthbert-Andersons know how to deliver a truly memorable performance!"

"Who's Mrs Tadworth?" Mum asked, which wouldn't have been my first question. I would probably have homed in on us using a real-life donkey in an amateur dramatics performance in a church.

"Vivian Tadworth is Minty's arch-nemesis," Grandfather said with a smile.

At this point, my brain was really struggling to keep up with what was going on.

"She is no such thing! A nemesis would suggest some sort of parity between us when there is no comparison! Mrs Tadworth is the terribly officious head of the local Women's Institute and the village council and I am Lady Cuthbert-Anderson!"

"That you are!" Grandfather said.

"Mrs Tadworth," Grandmother continued, "directs the nativities in the years we don't perform. I'll never forgive her for what she did to our show in 2016."

"What did she do in 2016?" I asked.

"She purposefully directed the organist I'd had flown over from Notre-Dame to a neighbouring church.

Margaret had to step in and play for us instead, and the dear tried her best but she just didn't have the skills necessary to match up with my vocal range. Oh, Reginald, imagine Vivian's face if we had a real-life donkey!" She turned to Dad. "Do go out and fetch the animal, Christopher. We can pop him in the stable block."

"You want me to go and fetch that donkey?" Dad said.

"Why, yes! Please do hurry before the pond overflows."

"I'll help too," Grandfather said, scooching his chair back.

Actually, storing the donkey in the stable for a bit wasn't a bad idea. I could keep it there while the Angel Gabriel and I went out scavenging for the other Bible characters. And if Mary and Joseph were as easy to find as their transport, I'd have them back trotting along the dusty road to Bethlehem in no time.

I stood up. "I'll give you a hand, Dad. Let's go before it tries to gallop away."

Grandmother reminded Grandfather that he was supposed to be taking it easy, but he insisted he would be fine. So off we went, completely confident of capturing the thing, with Molly following behind, shout-singing "Little Donkey" at the top of her lungs.

As it turned out, I later learned that donkeys aren't the galloping sort.

Even when the very existence of Christmas hangs in the balance and you try really hard to motivate them, they are still definitely more ploddy than gallopy.

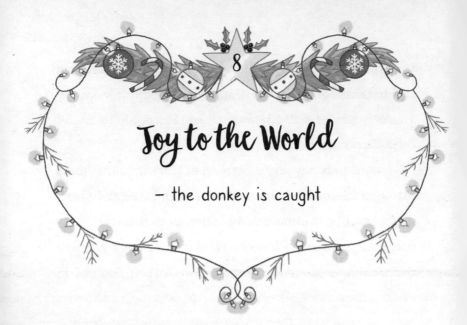

8

Joy to the World

– the donkey is caught

I was following Dad and Grandfather out to the back garden, wondering how easy it would be to actually catch a donkey with our bare hands, when I spotted something down the corridor and I almost let out a yelp of surprise. There he was, the Angel Gabriel in plain sight, with a look that I wouldn't exactly describe as angelic plastered across his face.

I flapped my arms, frantically motioning for him to hide. But he just stopped where he was and rolled his tea-cosied head to show that he was bored.

"The angel!" Molly cried.

I flapped my arms even more frantically and he threw

his arms in the air, clearly exasperated, then ducked into the nearest room just as Dad and Grandfather swung round to see what Molly was talking about.

"What was that, Molly-pops?" Dad said.

I gave her my *Keep your mouth shut* stare and I watched it slowly dawn on her that the Angel Gabriel was supposed to be a secret. She slapped her glittery-mittened hand to her forehead and said, "Nothing. There definitely-wefinitely wasn't an angel called Gabriel in the corridor. No, sireee!"

Dad smirked then turned back around. "Come on, you funny thing, let's go get this donkey."

I hissed to Molly, "We can't tell anyone, remember." Then I called after Dad and Grandfather, "I'll catch you up in two seconds."

I watched them disappear outside, then hurried into what turned out to be a little sitting room after the Angel Gabriel.

He was holding up a tiny figurine, looking at it with disgust. "What is this? Is this supposed to be me?"

"Yes. Now get your hands off, that's an antique, probably." I plucked it from his fingers and returned it to the nativity scene that was on display on a table.

"It looks nothing like me, I'm far more…luminous."

Yeah, very luminous, what with that tea cosy on your head, I thought. "Look, you need to get back to the toilet, where you're supposed to be!"

"I'm supposed to be in Our Father's heavenly kingdom, not a toilet."

"Well, you were the one who lost your powers and caused this mess. You need to go and wait for me there. If someone finds you wandering about, they'll think you're an intruder and report you to the police. You're not going to get Mary and Joseph back to Bethlehem from behind bars, now, are you?"

He flopped his arms down by his side and stuck out his bottom lip. "Fine."

"Are you sulking?"

"Nope."

"Well, good, because I actually have two bits of great news. Number one, I've a clue about the wise man—"

"Balthazar?"

"Yeah – if that's his name. I thought they were just called Wise Men One, Two and Three. But anyway, sounds like he was seen over at a George Budwell's place, so I say we start looking there."

"And the second bit of good news?"

"I've located the donkey."

The Angel Gabriel's face brightened. "Mary and Joseph's donkey?"

"I'm guessing there aren't too many stray donkeys round these parts."

He clapped his hands together. "This *is* good news! *Doubly* good news! I shall announce it to the world!"

He flung the door wide, opened up his wings – which whacked me right in the face – and managed to say, "Good n—" before I tackled him below the knees and brought him to the ground.

"You're supposed to stay hidden, remember?" I said. "So no announcing stuff!"

"Sorry," he said, clambering to his feet and shaking his wings. "Force of habit."

"You need to get yourself back to that bathroom and wait for me to come and get you. In the meantime, I'll find you some clothes which aren't quite so—"

"Magnificent?"

I looked him up and down. "Attention-grabbing. But first, I'm going to find out what is happening with this donkey. Don't get seen, okay?"

"You can trust me!" he said, nodding confidently. "I shall be completely inconspicuous!" He turned to leave the room and immediately got himself wedged in the doorway.

"Is there any way you can lose the wings for a bit?" I asked as I helped push him through. "They kind of don't help with the pretending-to-not-be-an-angel thing."

"There is…"

"Well, go on then. What are you waiting for… Christmas?"

"It is not, shall I say, a particularly enjoyable process."

"Do you know what else isn't a particularly enjoyable process? Having to hide an angel in your house because you have to help them save Christmas. Now get on with it and put them away."

"Fine! I shall endure the discomfort."

He bent over, put his hands on his knees and made a long grunting noise that sounded quite animal-y and went a bit like *"UGGG UGGGG EWWWG"*. He went cross-eyed and his nostrils flared so wide I was worried he might suck me up them. His cheeks flushed really red, he started panting and then, very slowly, his wings sort of contracted down inside him.

"Woah! Gabes, are you okay?" I said when it was finally all over.

"Fine, thank you very much for asking." He nodded curtly then walked out of the room with his head held high.

Outside, by the holly bushes at the back of the rose garden, I discovered a stand-off between Dad and Grandfather, and the donkey. While Dad and Grandfather were busy trying to catch the thing, Molly seemed otherwise engaged and was busy asking a robin that was sitting on the sundial whether it knew if it was going to snow soon.

"I told you, Molls," I said. "It never snows here at Christmas."

I walked over to Dad and Grandfather, who had successfully managed to back the donkey into the corner between the wall and the holly bush. Grandfather started swishing around the net that was used for cleaning the pond, like he meant to catch the donkey in it.

"Here, Oscar, you take this," he said, handing it to me.

I looked at the net, a bit confused about what they wanted me to do with it. It was no way big enough for donkey-fishing.

"Careful," Dad said, "in case he makes a run for it."

The donkey didn't look in the least bit like he was going to make a run for it. It just stood there looking very sullen and a bit bored. It had what seemed to be an old empty sack tied to its back – which I reckoned had come from biblical times.

Dad nodded at me. "Ready, Oscar?"

"Ready for what?" I said.

"Here goes…"

"Here goes what?"

"When I say…"

"When I say what?"

Dad didn't answer, he just bellowed, "NOW!" at me. And he bellowed it so urgently that I just went with my instincts and swung the net over the head of the donkey. The donkey didn't even move. It just stood there, looking completely unbothered and even more bored. And I stood there with a donkey's head in my fishing net.

"Oscar?" Dad said. "I was hoping you might use the stick to steer the donkey to the gate and into the stables."

"Oh," I said, not really knowing what the best course of action was now.

Grandfather grabbed hold of the rope which was tied around the donkey's neck and I took the fishing net off its head. Then Grandfather led it out of the rose garden and into the stable block, where my grandparents used to keep horses until their hips got too old for them to ride any more.

We shut the door and the donkey continued to stand there looking very bored and very unbothered.

Molly made an "EEEE-AWWW" noise and the donkey puffed some air out of its nostrils and turned its head away.

"He says his name is Donald," Molly told us.

Grandfather did a big chortly laugh. "Is that so?"

"Yup. I can speak to animals. I understand Donkilish."

"Donkilish?"

"Yup. Just like English but spoken by donkeys."

"I wonder if you can find out where he came from, Molly," Grandfather said.

He was obviously joking but Molly did another "EEEE-AWWW" sound. Donald made a big floppy raspberry noise with his lips. "He says he's over two thousand years old and he belongs to Mary and Jacob."

"Joseph," I corrected her and then realized that we shouldn't be giving away information like that, so I shouted out, "But clearly she's making that up. There is no way this donkey came from Nazareth."

Dad and Grandfather both gave me a look which said, *Well obviously, Oscar.*

Molly must have remembered that we weren't supposed to be telling anyone about what was going on, because she suddenly felt the need to say, "And there definitely isn't an angel in the loo either."

Grandfather said, "Goodness, this kind of nativity hysteria doesn't usually set in until *after* your grandmother has started rehearsals."

"I hope it goes smoothly this year," Dad said. "It would be nice to have a year without something going horribly wrong."

"Don't worry, Christopher. Your mother is most energized about the whole thing! I'm certain this year will be like nothing we have ever seen before."

He was very not-wrong about that.

"Yes, Minty's drawn up a strict rehearsal schedule," Grandfather continued. "She's going to keep us all very busy, but 'tis the season where we must play our parts, I suppose!"

Now this *was* a problem. I already had a part to play and a pretty massive one at that! I couldn't be memorizing lines when Christmas and me and the world as we knew it were under threat. I needed a plan. Well, a couple of plans, really. Not only did I have to work out how to get out of rehearsals unnoticed, I had to figure out how to locate Mary and Joseph and the wandering shepherd.

But the only plan I had at that point was to go and have a look for a guy running about in fancy clothes over at George Budwell's farm. Even then, there was no guarantee that the man he'd seen was Balthazar. And if he was, how was I actually going to catch him? I doubted fishing nets would work any better on a wise man than they had done on a donkey.

Saving Christmas, I realized, was not going to be easy. And with it already being the twenty-first of December, time was not on my side.

9

All I Want For Christmas

is a wise man, a shepherd, Mary, Joseph, and for my grandfather to be well. (And if there's room for anything else, a VR headset for my PlayStation.)

Before Dad and Grandfather went inside to inform the others that Donald was safely in the stable, I informed Dad and Grandfather that Molly and I were going exploring. Dad told us not to stray too far from the house. As he'd once said that nowhere was far away in Chipping Bottom, I took that as permission to go where we wanted. And after we'd collected the Angel Gabriel and got him out of the house without anyone noticing, our first destination would be George Budwell's farm.

With everyone downstairs, I told Molly to keep guard while I ran up to my parents' room and borrowed some clothes from Dad's suitcase. I also swiped a flat cap off one of the hooks in what Grandmother calls "the boot room", before slipping into the downstairs bathroom.

The Angel Gabriel rose from the toilet, in what might have been a majestic manner if it hadn't been for the tea cosy, and said, "Hallelujah! At last you arrive. I have been waiting atop this porcelain throne for long enough. We must commence the search for Mary and Joseph and the others at once!"

"First, you must put on some regular clothes," I said, passing him the bundle. "People will ask questions if you walk around looking so—"

"Splendid?"

"Angel-y."

He held up a pair of my dad's boxer shorts – they were his festive ones with the Brussel sprout pattern – and gave me a questioning look.

"For the sake of blending in, I will wear these unusual garments. Kindly step outside while I disrobe."

We did as he asked and waited outside the door until he said, "You may enter." When we went back in, he held his arms out and did a little spin. "What do you think?"

"Not bad," I said. I think I'd picked out the perfect jumper. It had a picture of Jesus giving a thumbs up and the words *Reason For The Season* on the front. Seemed quite fitting in the circumstances.

He still did look a little otherworldly with that luminous skin of his, but overall the new clothes worked.

"What do you reckon?" I asked.

"I mean, it will do, but..." The Angel Gabriel frowned then did a couple of lunges. "What *are* these? They're so uncomfortable and restrictive. Why would anyone wear such beastly things?"

"They're just jeans," Molly said.

"Why are Just Jeans so unyielding? My legs feel so claustrophobic. They're so rigid and scratchy..."

To be honest, he made a fuss for quite a long time but as nobody likes a whinger, I'll spare you the rest of the whingeing.

Once he was over his apparent horror at a pair of trousers, he spent a *long* time checking himself out in the bathroom mirror.

"I thought you wanted to get going?" I said.

"Tell me, are we settled on this hat? While I do admire the peak, don't you think the colour is a little...drab? I'm wondering if the jolly knitted one I had on before is more fitting for the messenger of God's words."

"The other one was a tea cosy," I said.

He looked at me blankly.

"It goes on a teapot to keep the tea warm," Molly explained.

"Are you a teapot?" I asked.

"What is a teapot?" the Angel Gabriel asked.

"A pot which you put tea in."

"I'll stick with the green-and-brown check."

"Fabulous. Now, as the important matter of your headwear is settled, let's go. We're going to head across the fields to George Budwell's place. That's where I think the wise man fell from the sky. I reckon if there are any clues to be found as to where he is, the barn would be a good place to start."

We put on our scarves and Molly tugged up her glittery mittens, then we slipped on our wellies because the fields would be quite muddy. The Angel Gabriel had very dainty feet, so I gave him Mum's to wear, but when he saw Molly's gold sparkly ones, he had a bit of a sulk that his weren't as wondrous.

"I just think if anyone is wearing the glittery wellies it should be the angel not a girl dressed as a unicorn," he told me when I asked what the big deal was.

When he wasn't going on about that, he kept moaning about the chafing from the Just Jeans. Who knew an angel could be quite such a moan-pot?

Anyway, we eventually made it out of the house and across the fields, despite Molly stopping repeatedly to question the sheep about whether they had seen a wise man anywhere and to examine the sky for signs of snow.

"She doesn't think the sheep can understand her, does she?" the Angel Gabriel asked as we stood back and watched her shouting at a sheep to tell her all it knew because she had ways of making it speak.

"I don't know what goes on in that brain of hers."

"She's quite the interrogator."

Molly shook her head. "These guys don't know anything. Let's go!"

We carried on, over a gate and along a narrow lane, until we came to a farm which we correctly assumed belonged to George Budwell.

"What now, Osky?" Molly asked. "Want me to go and question those cows?"

"Not a *bad* idea, Molly, but I was thinking we might just speak to George Budwell himself rather than the livestock. Find out what he saw exactly. He might be able to tell us what direction the wise man ran off in."

We didn't need to knock on the farmhouse door because George Budwell must have spotted us and had come outside to see what we wanted. He was a very square-shaped guy, with shoulders as broad as he was tall and a large red nose which, for some reason, I had a strong urge to go up and squish. I didn't though, obviously.

"Can I help you folk?" he said, stuffing his hands into his pockets.

"You wear Just Jeans too!" the Angel Gabriel announced.

George Budwell looked rightly confused.

"We wanted to ask you about what happened last night – to the roof of the barn," I said.

"News round here certainly travels fast!" he chuckled. "My Nancy should have a prize for how quickly she can spread the word on things."

"If anyone should get a prize for announcing things, I believe it should be me," the Angel Gabriel said. "I am the one who announces."

George Budwell looked rightly confused again.

"So what happened?" I asked, keen to get on with what we were supposed to be doing.

"Never seen anything like it. There was this flash of light so bright it lit up the whole bedroom and then I heard an almighty bang, so I stuck my head out the window and heard someone groaning loudly. That's when I noticed the hole in the barn roof. I stomped outside, shouting for whoever it was to get off my land."

"What happened then?" I asked.

"Well, they didn't seem keen to meet an angry farmer in his underpants and took off over those fields there, towards the woods."

We all turned to see the woods. They looked exactly like a place a travelling wise man might choose to hide, I decided.

"What did he look like, this man?" I asked.

"Did he look very wise?" Molly asked.

"Wise?" George Budwell frowned.

"Yeah, like an owl," Molly said.

"You're asking me if he looked like an owl?"

"What we mean is, could you describe him?" I said.

"Difficult to get a good idea of what he looked like, what with it being dark and him retreating yonder, but I said to my Nancy at the time he looked quite...fancy. He was wearing long robes and this hat-type thing. Could have been in fancy dress, I 'spose. He was clutching hold of something too. Couldn't see what, mind you. My reckoning is that it was probably some dafty messing about. Some dafty who has left me with a great big hole to patch up."

"Thank you, Mr Budwell, you have been very helpful."

"Say, aren't you the Cuthbert-Anderson lot?"

"Yup," Molly said.

"Tell your grandmother I'll be dropping something round to yours tomorrow. She won first prize in Mrs Tadworth's Women's Institute raffle in aid of the church roof and I'm delivering her winnings."

"Okay," I said, not thinking much about it at the time. Funny how things that seem of absolutely no importance can one day show up and savagely launch themselves at you when you least expect it.

We waved goodbye to Mr Budwell and headed off towards the woods, hoping that we would find a wise man amongst the trees and be one step closer to sorting out the Angel Gabriel's mess before Christmas Eve – which was now in only three days and about fourteen hours' time!

10

Four calling birds, three French hens, two turtle doves

and a wiseman in a fir tree

"Balthazar, Balthazar, if you are there, reveal yourself this instant! I command it!"

The Angel Gabriel had been shouting into the woods for a good twenty minutes. Molly had quickly grown bored and was off whacking toadstools with a stick. If the wise man who went by the name of Balthazar was hiding among the trees, it was pretty obvious to me that he didn't want to come out. Frankly, I didn't blame him. The Angel Gabriel had grown increasingly terrifying the longer his calls were unanswered, which I don't think was helping.

"You might want to try and sound less...threatening," I suggested.

The Angel Gabriel turned to me, a look of bewilderment etched on his face. "Whatever do you mean?"

"You've literally just threatened to rain down fire and brimstone on all that he loves if he doesn't show himself. I don't think I'd be that motivated to come out and meet the person who had bellowed that at me. So you might want to try and be a little more encouraging...friendly, even. The poor guy has been blasted two thousand years into the future. He's probably scared."

The Angel Gabriel rolled his eyes in what Mum would describe as a petulant manner. "Fine." He cupped his hands around his mouth and hollered, "Balthazar, great wise man, show yourself or I shall rain fire and brimstone down on you and all that you love, *please*? There..." He nodded at me. "How was that?"

"How's that?" I said. "Well, I'll be staggered if he doesn't come skipping out of the forest into your open arms."

"Really?"

"No, not really." I checked my watch. "We'd better

not be too much longer or someone might notice we're missing. I think we should spread out and scour that part of the wood over there. If we haven't found him by lunchtime, I suggest we come back later and have another look."

I called to Molly, who was aggressively hitting a patch of puffball mushrooms. My shout startled her so much that the stick flew clean out of her hands, and she spent a moment looking about, wondering where it had gone. "Come on, Molls, we're going to check over there."

She came skipping up to me and stuck her mittened hand in mine. We walked further into the wood, but there was still no sign of a wise man.

I was about to suggest heading back when Molly noticed something at the foot of a tree.

"What's that, Osky?" she said.

It looked like a big silver gravy boat with a lid, which was an odd thing to find out in Chipping Bottom woods. I bent over, picked it up and lifted off the top. A *very pungent* smell wafted up my nostrils. "Blimey!" I said. Inside was what looked like, on first inspection, a load of small brown stones.

"What *is* this stuff?" I held out a handful. Molly gave

a sniff so big that I was worried one of the stones might disappear up her nose like the terrible lost grape incident of 2019.

The Angel Gabriel loomed over my shoulder. "I believe that is myrrh. Balthazar is here somewhere!" He cupped his hands round his mouth again. "Balthazar, I know you are there! Show yourself."

"I always wondered what myrrh was," I said. "Seems like a really weird gift to give a baby. What even is it?"

"It's a fragrant resin," the Angel Gabriel said.

"What does a baby want with a fragrant resin?"

"Nothing, that's what! Just come out and say it! It's an inferior gift!" Suddenly someone dropped down from one of the trees. He was wearing robes of green, red and gold and had an incredible headdress on his head. He had the deepest brown eyes and was the second most magnificent person I'd ever seen, bearing in mind that I'd discovered the Angel Gabriel in his haloed brilliance only the night before.

"Ah, Balthazar, there you are. Hallelujah! Let us rejoice!" the Angel Gabriel said.

The look on Balthazar's face told me that he was not in the mood for rejoicing. I supposed he was annoyed that he'd fallen through a barn into some completely strange place and then been shouted at by at least two people.

However that, bizarrely, was not what he was primarily focussing on.

Later, when I asked him why he hadn't been traumatized by his sudden appearance in Chipping Bottom, Balthazar told me that people from his time were used to all sorts of unusual happenings. They'd grown up on a diet of stories about everything from floods to plagues of locusts, and angels, by all accounts, seemed to appear frequently. Which was why he was mainly upset about what he believed to be a great and terrible injustice.

"We'd agreed a price limit, which is why I went for the myrrh!" he shouted. "But what did they do?"

Molly and I took a step back; he seemed rather worked up.

I didn't know who *they* were or what they did, so I said, in what was admittedly a bit of a quivery voice, "Who are they and what did they do?"

"I'll tell you what they did! They double-crossed me, that's what they did! We'd all agreed a price limit, you know, so no one looked better than anyone else. But what happens? Caspar turns up on his camel with a load of frankincense and Melchior brings gold! And I'm sitting up there on my hump, holding myrrh, which is just, well, completely *bleurrrghhh* in comparison! Gold! I mean, that has got to have cost a fortune – it's *gold*!"

"Excuse me," I said, because I still had no idea how to respond or what he was really talking about. "Are you okay? You don't seem very okay."

"I just heard you! You said it yourself – *myrrh seems like a really weird gift to give a baby!*" He chose a rather high-pitched tone which was not an accurate or flattering impression of me.

"I...I...pfffffffftttt." I really didn't know how to respond.

"You didn't even know what myrrh is!"

"That's because I've never really needed any myrrh before."

"Exactly! And now I'm the one turning up at the birthday party of our Lord and Saviour with the rubbish present."

"You should get him a pirate-racoon puppet!" Molly blurted out. "That's what is top of my Christmas list!

128

Along with it snowing on Christmas Day, that is."

Balthazar, apparently noticing Molly for the first time, leaped backwards and yelled, "What is that thing?"

"It's a child in strange clothing," the Angel Gabriel said matter-of-factly. "She fooled me too the first time I met her."

"It's a unicorn onesie," I said.

"And it is nothing compared to her previous attire. Honestly, you should have seen her yesterday, dressed as a very strange beast. Most alarming."

Balthazar gasped and pressed himself back against a tree trunk. "Is she possessed...you know...evil? She has the most unnerving way about her."

Molly did a big harrumph. "I'm not evil! I'm a little angel, that's what I am!"

"You are definitely not an angel." The Angel Gabriel sounded almost insulted.

"I am. My daddy told me so. And look—" She turned around and waggled her arms. "See those lumpy bits on my back? That's where my wings are going to grow from."

"That's not where wings grow from!" the Angel Gabriel said, looking completely horrified.

"Well, they're not going to grow out of my bum, are they?" Molly said. She's very sarcastic for someone her age. I blame Mum.

"Do you think," I said, trying to get the conversation back on track, "we should tell Balthazar what's going on and discuss what happens next?"

"A good suggestion, but I can tell you with absolute certainty that *next* will not involve your sister sprouting wings from her scapulae."

"As I said, why don't we move on and focus on Operation Save Christmas – you know, the time on Earth when there is peace and goodwill to all men—"

"And chocolate oranges in your stocking and reindeers on the roof," Molly added.

"Yes, those too. And remember that bit you mentioned about the importance of ensuring the arrival of the baby Jesus?" I said pointedly to the Angel Gabriel. "I really think we need to figure out where we go from here."

I turned to Balthazar. "To get you up to speed: basically, back in zero BC – that's the time you came from – when the Angel Gabriel announced that Jesus was going to be born unto Mary, he got a teeny bit carried away in the power stakes and accidentally transported

131

you, a shepherd, Mary and Joseph and definitely a donkey through space and time. We need to get you all back to Bethlehem before irreparable damage is done."

"Righty-oh," Balthazar said, which was a little surprising. I was expecting him to ask a couple of questions at least, but he seemed to take it all in his stride. "Do you think there will be time for me to stop off at a gift shop before we return? I really would like to get this present situation sorted." He nodded at Molly. "You, child, tell me where I can find one of the racoon-pirate puppets. Is it a gift fit for the holy saviour of the world?"

"Yeah, definitely!" Molly said. "I love its big goggle eyes!"

I put the myrrh gravy boat under my arm. "I think we'll keep hold of this just in case."

11

Tis the Season

to keep a close eye on your cousins in case they mess things up for you

One of the benefits of staying in a house that is so big is that it isn't too difficult to hide an angel and a wise man without anyone noticing. If Molly and I had tried the same thing at home, Mum would have definitely realized we were up to something.

On the way back from the woods, we questioned Balthazar some more. Unhelpfully, he had no idea where Mary or Joseph or the missing shepherd were, but he agreed he would join the search to find them. I'll give him the benefit of the doubt and say it was because he knew it was the right thing to do and not because the Angel Gabriel had mentioned fire and brimstone again.

At that moment in time, despite the monumentally massive task ahead of us and Grandmother's rehearsals looming, I was feeling pretty positive.

"I think we're doing very well," I told the Angel Gabriel when Molly and I had installed him in the bathroom again. He had taken up his position on his "throne" and Balthazar was reclining in the bathtub. "We've already found Donald the donkey and Balthazar the wise man and we still have three and a half days until Christmas Day. You know, I'm feeling quite confident that we're going to do this."

Molly and I headed back into the main part of the house and found Grandfather in the entrance hall, carrying a basket of carrots.

"Ah, just the people. I'm going out to feed the donkey, would you like to assist?"

"You betcha!" Molly said.

Outside, Grandfather leaned over the stable door and gave Donald a rub on the nose.

"He really does need fattening up," I said. It was probably hard going for a donkey back in biblical times.

I climbed up onto a ride-on lawnmower that was parked beside the stable to get a better look. "Ooh, keys,"

I said, spotting them in the ignition.

"Don't get any ideas of driving that," Grandfather said. "Your mother was not very happy when I took you out for a spin in the Landy that time."

"I just love him! I've always wanted a donkey," Molly said, which was a desire she definitely had not dropped into any conversation before Donald showed up.

She tried to pull herself up so she could see over the stable door and get a better look at the holy ass, but she wasn't having much luck. I think it was the combination of wearing mittens and her lack of upper-body strength.

Grandfather said, "Let me help you out there," and lifted her up so she could see.

"Higher, Grandpops, higher! I want to kiss him!" Molly shouted, but after a few moments Grandfather put her down. He'd gone a bit grey in the face and had to steady himself against the wall.

"You okay?" I asked.

"Fine, young man. Probably just too old to be lifting up unicorns!" He laughed, but he really didn't look at all well.

Molly didn't notice what was going on. She was busy

135

taking a carrot from the basket and trying to throw it over the stable door, but instead it looped upward then dropped down and bonked Grandfather on the head.

Molly didn't notice that either and grabbed another carrot to hurl over, only to do the same thing again.

For a moment, I was genuinely worried that she'd finished Grandfather off with a couple of root vegetables, but while Grandfather didn't look any better, it didn't look like the carrot attack had made him any worse.

"I will love you for ever, Donald!" Molly yelled, then launched a third carrot at the donkey. This one made it over the door, bounced off the back wall and landed at his feet. Donald bent down and started munching.

"He says he loves it!" Molly shrieked and, before anyone could stop her, she grabbed the rest of the carrots and lobbed them over too. Poor Donald was pelted by the lot, but he didn't seem to mind. In fact, he seemed quite indifferent about everything going on around him. He just carried on lazily chomping away.

You would have thought that the most famous donkey after Eeyore would have a bit more...personality. But Donald seemed to be very lacking in any charisma at all.

Grandfather clapped his hands together. "Right, let's

head indoors and find out what your grandmother has planned for this afternoon rehearsal of hers."

I could really have done without the additional stress of the play, but part of me was still quite interested in the whole thing. It was a Cuthbert-Anderson tradition, after all, and as Grandfather was involved, I wanted to be too.

"I wonder what parts we'll be given," I said. "I played a bale of hay in the school nativity. That isn't even a living thing. I didn't get any lines and they made me sweep the stage after because I'd made such a mess."

Molly counted on her fingers. "I want to be a sheep or a camel, or the wise man that brings the pirate-racoon puppet."

"Do you know," Grandfather said, "I do not think I know about him."

"You can meet him if you like," Molly said.

Grandfather just ruffled her hair and said, "You really are such a wonderfully funny thing!"

Back inside Barlington, we were greeted by the noise of my grandmother hollering from up on the landing. I wasn't sure who she was bellowing at to start with, but then I realized she was leaning over the balustrade and running through her lines to an invisible congregation.

137

"Bravo, darling," Grandfather said, breaking into a round of applause. "A very stirring delivery. Mrs Tadworth has nothing on you, old girl!"

"I'm going to marry Donald because I love him," Molly said.

"What is the child talking about, Reginald?" Grandmother asked.

"She is rather smitten with the donkey, my dear."

"I'm not sure that is something to be encouraged," Grandmother said, then made a hushing sound. "Is that the sound of a car on the drive?"

Grandfather opened the front door. "I do believe that is James's lot arriving. It's all go in this house!"

He didn't know the half of it.

Molly and I stood on the front steps with our grandparents and Mum and Dad and watched our cousins, Fenella and Hugo, climb out of their black Range Rover. They were dressed in matching outfits: Hugo in khaki chinos, a blue sweater and white shirt, and Fenella in a pleated navy skirt and white shirt and blue jumper. On their feet were the shiniest shoes I have ever seen. Fenella's hair tumbled down her back in blonde ringlets, but the curls I remembered Hugo having had been replaced by a big floppy blond quiff. It reminded me a bit of a Mr Whippy ice cream and I had a sudden and overwhelming urge to stick a chocolate flake on his head.

The clouds actually parted at that moment and, I swear to you, a ray of light beamed down from the sun and illuminated Hugo and Fenella like they were actual angels.

"Oh yes, yes, you look positively perfect," Grandmother said, nodding with an admiration that hadn't been present for my and Molly's arrival.

Molly ran up to them, flipped back her unicorn hood, looked them up and down and, clearly impressed by what she saw, said, "Oooh la laaaaa! *Fancy!*"

Uncle James climbed out of the driver's seat and put his sunglasses on top of his head. He looks a lot like Dad, just tidier around the edges and a bit taller. Uncle James was wearing pretty much the same outfit as Hugo, which was a bit weird. If Dad started copying my clothes, I'd definitely have a word with him about it. There's no way he could pull off all-over camouflage print like I can.

"Little brother!" Uncle James said like he was making an announcement.

"Older brother!" Dad replied and jogged over to the car, and they shook hands then hugged.

"Good to see you, Christopherson!" Uncle James said, patting my dad's back.

"You too, Jimmy," Dad said. "Been a while."

"Too long," Uncle James said.

Aunty Marigold got out of the car too and wafted her free hand at us briefly as a hello. She seemed busy. Her mobile phone was clamped to her ear and she was saying, "Sell them, sell them now, or you'll be looking for a new job in the New Year, Marcus!" She laughed when she said that, but there was an edge to it. If I was Marcus, I'd shift whatever he needed to shift and fast. Aunty Marigold is what Mum calls a "power dresser". Her hair was all bouncy and curled under at the ends like a shell. She was even wearing lipstick. I don't think Mum even owns lipstick. Unless Vaseline counts.

"*Maman!*" Uncle James said, approaching Grandmother with his arms spread wide.

"It is wonderful to see you, James! Darling, you look so well!" Grandmother said, as she grabbed his shoulders and kissed his cheeks in turn.

"Fret not, Mother, number one son has arrived and we are ready to rally the troops for what will be the nativity performance of the decade – no, scrap that, the century!"

"Oi! Dad said. "I heard that."

"You were supposed to," Uncle James said and laughed this big laugh.

Whenever my uncle and Dad meet up, they always spend a lot of time pretending to be mean to each other like that. They do love each other but they are also a bit competitive.

"I'm so glad you're here, James!" Grandmother said.

"It will all be okay, Mummy," Uncle James said, giving her shoulder a squeeze.

Marigold finished speaking to Marcus, who I have never met but still feel a bit sorry for, and said to Mum, "Cathy, you look divine." Then she linked her arm through Mum's and said, "We'll get through this together, you and I, with lots of eggnog."

This is when Mum noticed the Christmas cake that I'd left on the ground next to Colin the campervan. "Oscar," she said, "I put you in charge of that. It's been outside all night!"

Dad went over and picked it up. The expression on his face when he lifted it showed he was surprised at how heavy the thing was. "Look, Mother," he said, lumbering towards her with it, "Cathy baked you a Christmas cake."

"Goodness," was all Grandmother said.

"Oh, it's probably ruined now," Mum said. "What a waste! Three kilograms of dried fruit went into that."

Grandmother cast her eyes over the transparent

cake box. "I shouldn't think so, dear. That thing looks indestructible." Then she clapped her hands and said, "Now, let us all head inside, there is much to be done! We have a nativity to rehearse!"

There *was* a lot to be done.

Yes, I had a nativity to rehearse to keep Grandmother happy, but more crucially I had some very important people to get home and the world to save and I was one shepherd and a Mary and Joseph short. If I ever wanted to decorate another gingerbread house, or pull another cracker and marvel at the tiny tape measure inside, or just experience that festive family feeling that only comes once a year, I'd have to get going and save Christmas.

But first, there was the rehearsal, and I couldn't see a way out of it.

As we headed inside, Grandfather said, "I say, isn't this all jolly wonderful?" Then he rubbed his hands together like he was having the best time. "It will be lovely to watch all the cousins playing together."

Fenella and Hugo looked Molly and me up and down and we did the same to them, like a Wild West stand-off. Let's just say, I wasn't getting a warm fuzzy vibe off them. I hoped Fenella and Hugo weren't going to get in the way of Operation Save Christmas and mess things up. At that moment, they looked like just the sort who might sabotage any chance of peace and joy on Earth.

12

Bless all the dear children in thy tender care

— although I understand if you have second thoughts about Hugo and Fenella

Molly and I helped Hugo and Fenella up to the nursery with their many, many bags. When we got into our room, Fenella flopped down on her bed and said, "I wish we were going skiing."

"It's going to snow here, then you can ski," Molly said.

"It won't snow *here*," Fenella said. "Not in a million Christmases! Ugh, it's going to be soooo boring!"

"It's not boring!" Molly said, grabbing her lightsaber off her bed and swishing it about wildly. "We found an angel and a donkey *and* a wise man. We're keeping them in the loo. Well, not Donald, he's in the stable."

"What on *Earth* are you talking about?" Fenella said, her face curled up in a sneer.

"Nothing! Molly's always coming out with weird stuff. She's got a big imagination, that's all," I said, then whispered to Molly, "as well as a massive mouth."

"Very odd," Fenella said.

She was looking Molly up and down in a way I didn't like, so I said, "There is a donkey in the stable though – she's right about that."

Molly positioned herself on her bed so that her head was on the floor and her legs were on her pillow and pointed her lightsaber at Fenella. "He came here all the way from Bethlehem!"

"Is she right about that too?" Hugo said, but it wasn't an actual question because he didn't look like he was interested in an answer from me. Bit rude. But also good, in that I didn't have to straight up lie to his face.

"I just don't know why we had to come here," Fenella said in a very whiney voice. "This whole nativity show thing is so stupid."

"You know why," Hugo said, hanging up a blazer in the wardrobe. "Grandfather's sick."

Molly bolted upright, her cheeks pink from where

the blood had rushed to her face. "What do you mean? Why did you say Grandfather is sick, Hugo?"

"I said he's sick because he *is* sick," Hugo said. "*Very*, apparently."

I scowled at him. Molly was too young to understand, and I didn't want her to get upset.

"Grandfather said himself he's fine, Molly, so don't worry."

"He's not fine. He's dying. You shouldn't lie to her," Fenella said.

Molly's eyes grew wide. "Dying? Like, he will be dead, like Harold-dead?"

"Like who-dead?" Fenella asked.

"Harold-dead. Harold was her goldfish," I explained.

"Well, yes then. Grandfather will be dead like Harold your goldfish," Fenella said, very matter-of-factly, but I caught the look in her eye. She tried to hide it, but I could tell she was sad too. I suppose that's how some people deal with stuff – by pretending it doesn't hurt in the hope that it won't.

Hugo cleared his throat, then forced a laugh. "But don't worry, we won't flush Grandfather down the loo when the time comes."

"That's really not funny," I said, and he looked away, like he knew he'd gone too far. "You shouldn't even joke about flushing old people down the loo."

"Or fish! I didn't flush Harold down the loo! I could never do such a thing!" Molly squealed. "I put him in my special shoebox under my bed with all my other treasures."

"Harold's under your bed!?" I said.

"*Who* is under your bed?"

We all looked around to see Grandfather, standing in the doorway and looking slightly bemused.

I blushed, worried about how long he'd been standing there. I hoped he hadn't heard Hugo talk about flushing him.

"Just some dead fish," Hugo replied.

"Harold wasn't *just some dead fish!*" Molly said, jumping up and pointing her lightsaber under Hugo's chin. "Harold was the best fish in the world."

"I'm sure he was, my unicorn queen!" Grandfather said.

"The best," Molly repeated, and snarled at Hugo, who seemed completely unfazed by her bared teeth.

Grandfather chuckled. "If you're all settled in here,

your grandmother wants to see everyone down in the drawing room to discuss our nativity roles. We can't sit around here chitter-chattering – I'm an old man, you know. Won't be long before the time comes when I'm to be flushed away by my dearly devoted grandchildren."

He spoke with a smile, but both Fenella and Hugo looked a little shamefaced about what they'd said. I certainly felt bad.

As we walked down the big stairs to the drawing room, Molly tugged Grandfather's sleeve and I heard her say, "Don't worry, I won't let them flush you. There's a big box in the garage that the washing machine came in. I'll put you in that instead."

While the others made their way to the drawing room, I snuck down the corridor to go and check on the Angel Gabriel and Balthazar and to promise them that I would get back to the search as soon as I could. No doubt they were getting worried and anxious.

I knocked lightly, then opened the door.

My eyes were assaulted by what they saw on the other side and I gasped. Loudly.

The Angel Gabriel was sitting on the closed toilet lid with his feet in a foot spa and a face pack on.

The shower curtain was drawn across the bath.

I shut the door behind me and hissed, "What are you doing? Is he...?"

The curtain shot back.

"Having the most wonderful time!" Balthazar said.

"You know you're supposed to take your clothes off?" I said.

He shrugged, then lifted up a very old-looking bottle of bubble bath. "What is this magical potion? What are these delightfully fragrant puffs of air? I have never felt so clean!"

I was too stunned to answer for several moments. Eventually I said, "It's just lavender bubble bath."

"Then this *just lavender bubble bath*," he said, looking at the bottle like it was the most wonderful thing he had ever laid eyes upon, "shall be what I gift to the baby king, our Lord Jesus Christ, on the day of his birth!"

"Bubble bath?" I said. "For Jesus? I'm sorry, what?"

"It will be a far greater treasure than either gold or frankincense! Do either of those give you soft supple skin and…" He read from the label on the back. "…make you feel as though you are unfurling a blanket in the long grass and savouring a warm breeze that carries the sweet scent of lavender?"

"I imagine they do not," I said.

"Exactly! It is perfect!"

This whole time, the Angel Gabriel was leaning back on the toilet, eyes closed and still wearing the flat cap so his halo didn't act like a Belisha beacon and notify everyone to his whereabouts.

"This is heavenly," he said. "My already radiant skin shall be even more radiant!"

"And he's the one to know about radiance!" Balthazar said. Then he plopped a great big dollop of bubbles on his own head and began to give himself a scalp massage.

"Right…I think I might just leave you guys to it. I'll come back later and we can go and have a look for Mary, Joseph and that shepherd."

"Steve, his name is Steve," the Angel Gabriel said with a lazy, happy sigh.

"Okay, you two hang out here, doing whatever it is that you're doing, and I'll head back so we can find Mary, Joseph and Steve later."

Balthazar said, "Don't rush," then slid down under the water level, his clothes billowing out around him.

I closed the door to the bathroom and made my way down the corridor to Grandmother's rehearsal, still not quite believing what I had got myself into, and not knowing if I was going to be able to sort the whole merry mess out. But one thing I did know was that while the Angel Gabriel and Balthazar were different to anybody I had ever met before, I was starting to really like them. I didn't want to just save Christmas for me, but for them too.

13

Hark! the herald angels sing

– or bellow, if Grandmother is acting

I nside the drawing room, Grandmother was holding a pointing stick and standing next to a flip chart. I knew then that the woman meant business.

"Please, take a seat," she said, waving the stick towards the sofas. "There is an awful lot to get through. Marigold, if you wouldn't mind ending your telephone conversation."

Aunty Marigold rolled her eyes, sighed and reluctantly ended her phone conversation by shouting at that guy Marcus again.

We all sat down on the various sofas and chairs. Molly sat cross-legged on the floor.

"I truly believe that this year's nativity will be one to remember," Grandmother began.

Grandfather walked over and took my grandmother's hand and kissed it. "With you at the helm, old girl, I have no doubt it will be a huge success."

Grandmother blushed a little. She didn't take her hand from Grandfather's for several seconds. They looked at each other like they had forgotten that anyone else was in the room. It dawned on me right then just how much they loved each other. It was quite a nice moment.

Until Molly ruined it by doing an enormous "BAAAAAAA!"

Everyone looked at her in surprise.

"I want to be a sheep from the Bible," Molly said by way of explanation and began moving across the rug on all fours.

Grandmother clutched her hand to her chest. "That sound you just emitted really is not, by any stretch of the imagination, biblical."

Molly stopped scrambling about on the floor and looked up, confused.

"I think the sheep dream is dead in the water, Molls," I told her.

She looked like she was considering this for a moment. Then she lifted her big eyes up towards Grandmother and said a hopeful, "Rooooarrr?"

"What in the nativity story roars?" Hugo spluttered.

"A camel, of course!" Molly said.

"Camels do not roar, darling," Mum said.

Grandmother flipped over the first page of the chart to reveal a title: *Cast List*. She pointed her pointy stick at Molly's name and shook her head. "No animals. You are to be an angel, along with Fenella and Hugo."

Molly huffed and crossed her arms and generally looked quite annoyed about being an angel. To be honest, I thought that it would take a vast amount of acting skill for Molly to pull that one off.

My eyes trailed down the list until I found my name. "Shepherd!" I said.

"A very important role. I'm sure you can find it in you to deliver a convincing performance," my grandfather said and gave me a wink.

What I really needed to find was the actual shepherd, Steve, but I was secretly a bit thrilled to have a part that was an actual human being, rather than animal feed!

"Am I going to get any lines?" I asked.

"Yes, you have been allocated lines – whether you shall deliver them will be determined by your attitude in rehearsals. An actor must earn the right to speak, Oscar," Grandmother said.

"I see you are the Angel Gabriel, Mother," Dad said, flashing Mum a cheeky grin.

"Correct, and the narrator of the play. This year, I shall forgo the role of Mary," Grandmother said.

"Because you're a very old lady and Mary was a beautiful donkey princess?" Molly said.

"Mary was nothing of the sort! She was the blessed Holy Mother! And it has nothing to do with age, child!" Grandmother scoffed. "A good actress can portray a range of characters of varying years. My Mary was described as both convincing and compelling in the *Village Post*. No, this year, I will stand down because your Aunty Camilla is with child, and I believe that will lend some artistic integrity to the whole performance. Who knows, perhaps she may even give birth during the play!"

"Goodness, I sincerely hope she doesn't," Dad said, and I don't think I've ever agreed with something so strongly.

"Christopher, you shall be another shepherd. Reginald, James and Geoffrey the gardener will be the three kings, naturally. And as he is Camilla's beau, I have cast Patryk as Joseph – one can only hope he is up to the part. I'm not sure if he has a great deal of acting experience. Marigold will be the innkeeper, and I think that's it."

"I don't have a part," Mum said, and although she had done nothing but moan about the whole nativity thing, she sounded a bit put-out.

"Cathy, you will be the *extras*."

"Extras *plural*?" Mum said, arching an eyebrow.

"Yes, the other innkeepers, perhaps a shepherd, nothing too taxing. I am well aware the creative arts are not your forte."

"She's pretty good at baking," I said. "I don't know anyone who can make a cake as heavy as hers."

"Quite. But alas, there is no baker in the nativity story," Grandmother replied, then opened a drawer in the bureau, pulled out a pile of scripts and handed them out. "First task is for you to make yourselves familiar with the lines. Margaret has highlighted your parts. It is of the utmost importance you know your words completely, to allow me to direct you effectively."

Once we had our scripts, Grandmother stood in the middle of the room. Then she looked down at the floor and closed her eyes.

I wondered what was going on. It looked like her battery had just run out.

Suddenly she flung her arms wide and said, in a big booming voice, "And it came to pass, that in those days, there went out a decree from Caesar Augustus, that the whole world should be enrolled—" and I literally jumped out of my skin. Between you and me, the tiniest drop of surprise wee might have leaked out too.

"What's she doing?" I hissed to Dad.

"I believe she is acting, Osky."

"Oh, right. I didn't know it would be so loud."

Molly then piped up with, "The Angel Gabriel doesn't

sound *anything* like that! Have you got your angel impressions mixed up, Grandmother? Are you doing the Angel of the Worms or the Angel of the Boulder?"

Dad scooped her up and said, "Let's just quietly listen to Grandmother doing her thing."

You know, while it is lucky that everyone always thinks Molly is making things up, I do feel a bit sorry for her.

Grandmother regained her stride and continued with her lines. "This enrolling was first made by Quirinius, the governor of Syria..."

I looked down at my script – Grandmother's part was massive. I caught Dad's eye and he whispered, "Better get comfortable, buddy. This speech goes on a bit."

Mum did a massive yawn, which gave Aunty Marigold the giggles. She did her best to hide it, but it was too late; she'd set Mum off as well. Luckily, Grandmother didn't notice – she was too busy trying to be angelic.

She didn't even stop when Margaret burst into the room in a bit of a flap.

"Lady Cuthbert-Anderson," Margaret interrupted, I think quite bravely.

"What is it, Margaret?" Grandmother said, annoyed at being cut off for a second time.

"Oh, your ladyship, George Budwell has arrived at the front door."

"The farmer?" Grandmother said. "Why on Earth is he here?"

"He's delivering your prize from the raffle," Margaret said. "The one run by the WI to raise funds for the church roof."

Grandmother clapped her hands together. "Oh, how wonderful that we won. Please do show the poor man in. You can't leave him standing on the doorstep. Fetch him at once."

"I think you really ought to meet him at the door, Lady Cuthbert-Anderson," Margaret said, which I think everyone thought was a bit bold.

"You do, do you?" Grandmother raised an eyebrow.

Margaret gulped. "I do, Your Ladyship."

Grandmother rose from her seat. "Very well then, Margaret. Let us see what all the fuss is about."

I didn't mind what the fuss was if it meant the rehearsal might be over. I had a Steve and an expectant mother and her husband still to find – and smartish. I just had to have faith that it was possible, even though the hours were hurtling by.

160

14

On the first day of Christmas my true love gave to me

...a turkey?

I think everyone wanted to know why Margaret had a look of doom on her face, so we all followed Grandmother to the front door, where George Budwell was waiting. I knew I should get on with my other important role and check on the Angel Gabriel and Balthazar, but I didn't think it would take long and, really, how much trouble could they get up to in a bathroom?

George Budwell took off his flat cap when he saw Grandmother. "Your Ladyship." Then he spotted me and Molly and said, "Hello again, you two."

I thought Mum or Dad might ask what he meant by that, but I think everyone was too busy wondering what Grandmother had won.

Grandmother said, "Mr Budwell, a pleasure to see you. Margaret informs me that you wish to present me with my prize."

From the look on Margaret's face, I could just tell that the prize wasn't going to be a food hamper or an octopus, as Molly had randomly suggested to me on the way from the dining room.

Mr Budwell took a step to one side. "Here he is, isn't he a beauty?"

Fenella screamed and hid behind Aunty Marigold, saying something about being afraid of large birds.

Grandmother gasped, brought her hand to her chest and said, "Surely, there must be some mistake," which I think is what everyone else was thinking too.

Well, everyone except Molly, who shrieked, "He is even better than an octopus!"

Grandmother gave Molly a very odd look, but Molls didn't notice. She went right up to the cage that was on the ground behind Mr Budwell and said, "He *is* a beauty! I will love him for ever. Does he have a name?"

"A name?" Mr Budwell said, looking a bit confused. "No—"

Molly said, "I'll ask him," and bent down and made a *gobble-gobble* noise at the cage. Then she said, "Oh, that's sad, he says he doesn't have a name. In that case, I shall name him 'Grandma', because he has a wobbly neck just like she has."

Aunty Marigold and Mum both splutter-laughed at that.

Grandmother wasn't paying attention – she was probably too stunned by her prize.

"I won a turkey? A live turkey?" she said, her face a picture of horror. "What, pray tell, do you expect me to do with a live turkey, Mr Budwell?"

"Christmas is just around the corner, Lady Cuthbert-Anderson. I'm sure you'll be able to think of something," Mr Budwell said as he put his cap back on his head. "I must get back, the farmers' WhatsApp group has been lighting up this morning. Think there's a sheep poacher about. Someone's been spotted loitering in the fields. Although, no sheep have actually been taken. In fact, they seem to have been mysteriously fed..." he trailed off, deep in thought for a moment. "Wonder now if it's that fella who fell through my roof."

No one was interested in a sheep thief who wasn't actually stealing sheep, what with there suddenly being a large, slightly terrifying-looking turkey on the driveway. I think something in my head must have started whirring away without me knowing though, because the importance of what George Budwell had said came to me a bit later, during a rather unusual therapy session.

Anyway, George Budwell got back into his truck and drove off, leaving us with the crate containing the turkey version of Grandmother.

"What are we going to do with a live turkey?" Grandmother said again desperately.

"He can stay with us in the nursery," Molly announced. "The downstairs bathroom is already full of wise men and angels."

"No, he can't stay in the nursery," Mum said.

"It's Grandmother's house, it's up to her," Molly said, then clutched her hands together and did her big pleady eyes.

Unsurprisingly, they didn't work on Grandmother. She said, "Quite out of the question. Festive poultry has no place indoors, unless served with home-made cranberry sauce. Reginald, you will have to fetch Mr Budwell back and tell him he must take this thing away immediately!"

"I shall call him on the telephone, but in the meantime I suggest that we put it in one of the empty stables in the yard."

"Put him next to Donald so they can make friends and won't be lonely," Molly said.

Grandfather clapped his hands together. "A fine idea, young Molly."

"I'm certain this is all Mrs Tadworth's doing," Grandmother said, glaring down the path. "Imagine thinking that a live turkey would be an acceptable raffle prize!"

Uncle James and Dad and Grandfather each took a side of the crate and started to carry it across the courtyard, with Molly skipping along behind. Uncle James and Dad argued a bit about who should lead and which way they should go, so they took quite a zigzaggy path.

After a little while, Grandfather said, "Put it down. Put it down!"

I thought he'd had enough of their bickering, but then he bent over and clutched his hand to his stomach.

All the grown-ups started to panic. Mum called out, "Christopher, your dad!" and Uncle James said, "Oh, crikey!" and even Aunty Marigold stopped talking on her phone and looked alarmed for a moment.

Grandmother raced across to him, shrieking, "Reginald! Reginald! My Reginald!" in quite a dramatic manner.

Grandfather straightened up – well, he tried to. "It's all right, my darling. Don't fret. Just a twinge. No need to fuss." But I looked at his face, and I wasn't sure I believed him.

"Reginald, what on Earth did you think you were doing?" Grandmother shouted. "Hauling a turkey across the grounds? Christopher, why did you let him do that?!"

I don't think it was my dad's fault, but he didn't say that. He didn't say anything. He just stood there, staring at my grandad, looking suddenly very, very concerned.

"Margaret!" Grandmother bellowed. "Call Doctor Percival on the telephone and tell him to come here as a matter of urgency! I will not have my husband die at the hands of a turkey!"

Margaret dashed off inside and Grandmother continued to get herself in a right old flap.

Molly looked up to me, her forehead all wrinkled. "Osky, do turkeys have hands?"

"No, Molly," I whispered.

"But Grandmother said—"

"Not the time, Molly," I said and nodded towards Grandmother, who was now fanning herself with her hand and leaning on the turkey box.

"Oh goodness," Grandmother said. "I don't feel quite myself. This is all rather too much to cope with!"

"Mummy," James said. "Are you alright?"

"I...do...feel rather...unwell," she said, between large gasps for air.

Everyone suddenly seemed very concerned about Grandmother. Except Mum. I spotted her rolling her eyes and shaking her head, like she does when I make a fuss about tidying my room or Molly has a tantrum about not being able to wear her giraffe onesie to school.

Even Grandfather was asking her if she was okay and he was the actually-dying one.

Grandmother didn't say anything though, she just kept making loud gasping sounds, which were actually quite similar to the noise the turkey was making inside its box.

"She's hyperventilating," Aunty Marigold said, rushing across the gravel to her.

Grandmother stopped all the panting and barked, "I most certainly am not! I'm just breathing quicker than usual, that's all!" Then she started fanning herself again. "I think it's my blood pressure."

"Darling girl, are you alright?" Grandfather asked from his bent-over position.

Then Uncle James shouted at Dad, "Don't just stand there, go and get Mummy some water, *Christopher*!"

Dad said, "Why don't you go, *James*?"

And then they started arguing. Then Molly started crying because Hugo had told her we were going to eat Grandma for Christmas, so I had to give him a shove because he really deserved one. Then Fenella gave me a shove because she must have incorrectly thought I deserved one. And then

Molly gave her a shove and said, "Don't push my Osky!" It was a surprisingly hard shove and Fenella fell backwards and shrieked *really* loudly.

Aunty Marigold dashed over, pulled up a very snivelly Fenella from the floor and shouted at Mum to contain her "little savages". Apparently only Mum gets to call us "little savages" though – well, that's what she said to Aunty Marigold anyway.

By the time Margaret came out to tell us the doctor was on his way, there was a right scene unfolding on the front driveway.

Which very quickly quietened down when Hugo shouted, "Look! She's only gone and let the turkey out!"

And Molly shouted, "Fly, Grandma, FLY!"

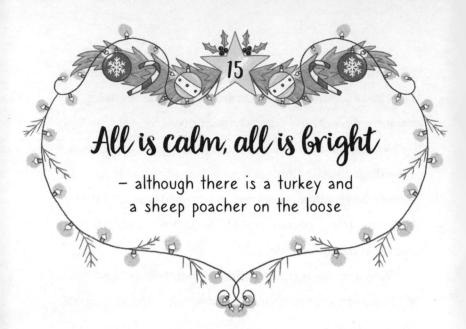

All is calm, all is bright

– although there is a turkey and
a sheep poacher on the loose

By the time Doctor Percival had arrived at Barlington, Grandmother's blood pressure had returned to normal, which she said was remarkable considering there was a turkey prowling about the grounds.

Doctor Percival told us all that we needed to stop Grandfather from overexerting himself and that we had to keep an eye on him. Grandfather, however, said that he was feeling much better and that he was absolutely fine.

"So no need to get your washing-machine box ready just yet, young Molly!" he had chuckled and I had tried to laugh too, but I mainly felt a bit sad and worried about him.

Grandmother went for some rest in her room, so she'd be ready to take us all carol-singing later. She said carolling would be a good chance for us to run through the hymns that we would be singing in the nativity. Mum told me and Molly that once we got back she wanted us all to make mince pies and biscuits to hang on the Christmas tree together like we usually do.

I tried to get out of it. "Do we have to?"

"Yes, you have to. It's a family tradition and just because we're here doesn't mean that we're going to miss it. I don't care what the rehearsal schedule says. This is my thing and we're doing it whether you like it or not. But you'd better like it."

When all the adults went off to do some adulting things somewhere, and poor Margaret was left with the job of tracking down Grandma turkey, I snuck along to the closed-off side of the house to see what was going on in the bathroom. I wanted to tell the Angel Gabriel and Balthazar about the plan I'd made to head off in search of Steve the shepherd the following morning. I thought we'd spread out around the village. It wasn't much of a plan, but it was something.

Thankfully, Balthazar and the Angel Gabriel were

now both out of their blissfully fragrant bubbles and fully dressed. Balthazar had wrapped what looked like one of Grandmother's very old frilly dressing gowns around him and the Angel Gabriel was lying in the now-empty bathtub, flat cap on, eyes closed. They appeared to be in the middle of some sort of therapy session.

I opened my mouth to ask what was going on, but Balthazar held up his hand and shook his head, so I closed it again.

"Please, Gabriel, go on," Balthazar said. "I feel like we're at a breakthrough moment."

"I suppose it's the worry of disappointing Him, you know? It's God, after all – you don't want to let the big guy down."

Balthazar nodded. "And tell me, Gabriel, what did the worry of disappointing Him lead to?"

"It led me to overdo my angel powers and accidentally transport some pretty important people into the future, thereby possibly altering the world quite dramatically by putting the birth of Jesus Christ in jeopardy."

"I think you need to let go of those feelings of not being good enough. Because you *are* good enough," Balthazar said. "You must work towards finding your own peace. Perhaps less of the fire and brimstone stuff, hey?"

"You really are very wise," the Angel Gabriel said as he sat up and wiped away a tear.

"Right, now that is over," I said, "shall we set our minds to sorting out peace on Earth as well? I've been thinking, where would you go if you were a shepherd?"

"If it was for a holiday," Balthazar replied, "I might be tempted by the draw of the Sea of Galilee. I hear it is very pleasant there in the spring."

I tried to figure out if he was being serious; by the look on his face, I guessed he was. Wise clearly meant something a bit different two thousand years ago.

"I meant if you were a shepherd who'd been accidentally transported to Chipping Bottom, where would you go?"

"I don't know, I'm not acquainted with the local beauty spots," Balthazar said. "Any sandy beaches in the vicinity? Could he have journeyed there for a little sojourn perhaps?"

Honestly, you'd expect more common sense from a supposed wise man, wouldn't you?

"I think if I was Steve," I continued, "I might be a

little scared, traumatized even, by what had happened. I'd probably want to hide somewhere." I slapped my hand to my forehead, because this is where my thoughts finally caught up with my brain. "Of course! That's it!"

They both looked at me blankly.

"George Budwell, the farmer, said earlier that a sheep poacher has been spotted around these parts."

"Focus, Oscar!" the Angel Gabriel said. "We need to think about where Steve might be. We cannot be distracted by the actions of George Budwell and sheep poachers."

I took a deep breath, like my teacher does when she is trying to explain percentages to me for the gazillionth time. "Look, what I'm saying is that if I was Steve, I'd want to go somewhere that seemed familiar to me, somewhere like a sheep field."

"Goodness," the Angel Gabriel said. "Steve must be careful! There is a sheep poacher about!"

"I'm saying Steve *is* the sheep poacher! Except I don't think he's poaching sheep, I think he's just...hanging out with them."

"Praise the heavens! You could be right," the Angel Gabriel said. "One thing shepherds do love to do is watch their flocks, especially by night and seated on the ground. In fact, that's *exactly* what Steve was doing when I showed up to speak to him."

"And glory shone around, I guess?" I said.

"Yes, it did rather...well, until I ramped up the power output and we all ended up here."

"So anyway, I think we should go out early tomorrow morning—"

"Why not now?" the Angel Gabriel asked.

"Tonight we're all expected to go carol-singing and then Mum wants us to make mince pies—"

"Of course, we wouldn't want the fact that Jesus Christ might be born in Chipping Bottom to get in the way of mince pies, now, would we?" the Angel Gabriel said.

"I know it's not ideal. Trust me, if I could get out of it I would, but Mum's laid the law down on this one. But tomorrow, dead early, we'll go out and search all the sheep fields. I'll get a map. I've got a feeling there are quite a few fields we'll need to cover."

"Maybe we should take Donald the donkey, to save our legs?" Balthazar suggested.

I smiled. "No, not Donald. I have a better idea than that."

That evening, during what Grandmother calls supper and we call tea, Uncle Patryk and Aunty Camilla arrived. They turned up in a tiny and really flash-looking sports car.

Patryk leaped out, looking very Christmassy in his green jumper and red trousers but clearly a bit harassed, and ran around to the passenger side. He proceeded to try and pull out Aunty Camilla, who looked like she was more than a bit stuck.

After a bit of tugging, and a lot of complaining from my aunty, she shot out of the car like a cork, then stomped about a bit, rubbing her bump and her back.

"You'll have to get rid of that when the baby comes, Millie," Dad said, gesturing to the car.

"Yes, I know, Christopher," she said, giving Dad a kiss. "I'm terribly sad about it – it's the focus of my next column actually."

"Get yourself a Range Rover," Uncle James said, then gave her a kiss too. "Superb machines."

Aunty Camilla made a groaning noise and rubbed her belly. "Why is pregnancy so uncomfortable?"

Uncomfortable? She should try sitting for five and a half hours with a ton of Christmas cake on her lap.

"Brave of you to come here so close to your due date," Mum said.

"It is rather," Aunty Marigold agreed. "I refused to go anywhere when I was expecting the twins."

"Just had to be here for Daddy," Aunty Camilla said and everyone nodded. Then she bellowed over to Patryk, "Bring in the luggage," and proceeded to waddle up the steps, announcing that she was desperate for the loo and that Uncle Patryk should have listened to her when she asked to stop at the last services and that he wasn't the one with a bowling ball sitting on top of his bladder.

"Lovely to see you looking so radiant, Camilla!" Grandfather called after her.

Molly hopscotched across the gravel towards Uncle Patryk and told him, "You're Joseph, but not the one who is lost in Chipping Bottom, we still need to find him."

Uncle Patryk grinned and said, "Is that so?" then put the huge suitcase he'd just dragged out of the car onto the ground. He crouched down so he was on Molly's level and held out his hand. "Hi there, Molly, lovely to see you again."

Molly looked at Uncle Patryk's hand, then leaned forward and kissed it. I don't think she knows about handshakes.

"Do you remember me?" Patryk asked. "I haven't seen you since my wedding, the summer before last. But you've got much taller since then."

"That is because I am very excellent at growing. You are the exact same size, though. I remember you, because you have smart hair that and very nice teeth," she said, prising his mouth open to get a better look. "They're almost as shiny as the Angel Gabriel's halo!"

Once Patryk and Camilla were settled in, Grandmother handed us our hymn sheets and we all wrapped up warm in our hats and scarves and headed off down into the village to go carol-singing. Everyone had tried to tell Grandfather to stay home and rest, but he insisted on coming too. Molly was given a Christmas hat to collect donations in to go towards repairing the church roof, which she seemed pleased about, but as we walked down the drive, she tugged on the bottom of my coat and looked up at me with big worried eyes.

"What's up, Molls?" I asked.

"Osky, I can't read all the words on the singing paper."

"Don't worry, you'll probably know some of the songs anyway, and if you don't, just tra-la-la along as best you can."

"Okay! I can tra-la-la!"

The first house we went to belonged to a Mrs Tricia Pennyworthy, the lady who ran the village post office. It was like a minefield even getting to her front door, because of all the Christmassy decorations in her garden.

"It looks amazing!" Molly said, and I had to agree.

All of the ornamental animals that covered Mrs Pennyworthy's lawn had been given Santa hats. There was also a large inflatable elf with long flapping arms and a LOT of flashing lights.

Before using the knocker, Grandmother said, "Now, do sing up and enunciate your words. Mrs Pennyworthy, as well as lacking in taste when it comes to garden design, is also terribly hard of hearing."

Mrs Pennyworthy came to the door with her hair in rollers and wearing a Christmas jumper which said *Single and Ready to Jingle* and said, "Oooh, lovely! Can

179

you do 'Rocking around the Christmas Tree'?" which didn't go down brilliantly with Grandmother.

We didn't sing that. Instead we did "Joy to the World", which I don't think Molly knew, but she tried her best to pick up the words. By the end she was doing a lot of tra-la-la-ing and bellowing out "Joy to the Worm" quite forcefully. I kept catching Dad's eye and we got the giggles every time we saw Grandmother's face when Molly mentioned the worm.

Mum and Aunty Marigold stood at the back, sort of singing, and Camilla leaned against the garden wall while Patryk rubbed her back. Typically, Fenella and Hugo were pretty good singers, if you like that warbly-churchy style they had going on. Grandfather was surprisingly good too – he had a deep, deep voice that sort of reverberated through your body and almost made your teeth feel like they might rattle themselves clean out of your gums. When he heard Molly singing about the worm, he joined in too, which made me beam. Grandmother was quite operatic in her approach, and apart from when she was frowning at Molly, she delivered her performance with what she later told me was "great gusto".

I could think of other ways to more accurately describe it.

When we were done, and Mrs Pennyworth had admitted to not hearing a thing because she had forgotten to turn on her hearing aid, Molly stepped forward with her hat and Mrs Pennyworthy dropped ten pounds into it.

Uncle Patryk gave Molly a piggyback to the next house and on the way Grandfather said, "Excellent, well done, everybody."

"Beautifully sung, Fenella and Hugo," Grandmother said, "and an interesting effort from Oscar and Molly. Now, this next house is Mrs Tadworth's so I really would like to give a more polished performance. Catherine, Marigold, please don't hide away at the back, it didn't go unnoticed. And Reginald?"

"Yes, my love?"

"Please stick to the correct words."

Grandfather winked at me and Molly. "Of course, my angel."

Mrs Tadworth's place was a very lovely-looking cottage with a thatched roof and an immaculate garden. A woman, with quite a bouffant hair-do pushed back with a green velvet headband, who I guessed was Mrs Tadworth, opened the door.

Molly shouted, "Seasons greetings! Are you ready to hear some singing?"

Mrs Tadworth clutched her pearls, and said, "Goodness, I don't know if I am."

"Don't mind my granddaughter, she gets a little over excited," Grandmother said.

"Araminta," Mrs Tadworth said, "what a pleasure to see you. I do hope Mr Budwell dropped off your prize."

"Yes, he did and we were thrilled with it, weren't we, Reginald?"

Grandfather said, "Oh, yes, delighted."

When we'd finished "Once in Royal David's City", Mrs Tadworth gave us a little clap and said, "Jolly good effort, I'm sure you'll all be at performance standard by the time of the nativity."

Molly marched up to her, thrust the Christmas collection hat under her nose and said, "Pay up then, missus."

Mrs Tadworth raised an eyebrow and put a pound in the hat.

As we walked up to the next house, I heard Grandmother say, "A pound, Reginald, she only gave a pound!"

Grandfather said, "That woman wouldn't know a good performance if it hit her between the eyes."

The next house was a little more generous, and grandfather's old golfing partner, Mr Chandra, gave us a twenty-pound note thanks to what he described a "wonderful and interesting interpretation of 'Good King Wenceslas'."

Once we'd sung at all the people in Chipping Bottom who were willing to open their doors to us, we headed home. I was ready for a bit of a sit-down, but, true to her word, Mum made us bake some mince pies and Christmas biscuits for the tree. I hadn't been that excited, but it was actually kind of fun. Sure, they were a little misshapen and I didn't get to drizzle the icing on the top because Molly had drunk most of it when Mum wasn't looking, but we'd made them together and Mum said that made them taste better.

While we hung the biscuits on the tree, we made everyone try a mince pie and the whole family agreed they were pretty tasty, even Grandmother, who had eyed hers quite suspiciously when Molly had plonked it in her hand. After the mince-pie eating, it was getting quite late and I was quite tired, what with carolling and chasing around after angels and wise men and turkeys all day, so I wasn't too bothered when us kids were sent up to bed. Grandmother said that breakfast was to be a 'casual affair' the following morning and that she had organized for Margaret to leave out a platter of pastries for us and we were free to dine at our leisure. She had errands to run in the morning, but she expected us all present when she got back for our first complete run-through of our lines.

This was excellent news because it meant that Molly and I would have time to scour the fields for Steve first thing without being missed. Once we had him, it was only Mary and Joseph left to find. Although I was a bit worried about that, they were the most important ones after all. Tomorrow would be the twenty-second of December, which meant we only had three days to save Christmas and I hadn't the first idea where to even start looking for them. It was all very well having a wise man, but without Mary there would be no birth of Jesus. If I ever wanted to go carol-singing with my family or make mince pies with Mum and Molly again, I knew I had to come up with an idea pretty quickly.

Ho! Ho! Ho!

Who'd be a turkey at Christmas?

The following morning I woke up really, really early. There were only two days until Grandmother's nativity, and three days until I had to put everything right and make sure Jesus was born in Bethlehem two thousand years ago instead of in twenty-first century Chipping Bottom, in order to save me, Christmas and... well, you get the drift. Festively speaking, I was up against it.

I tippy-toed over to Molly's bed and gave her a little shake. "Get yourself dressed quietly, we're going out to search for Steve this morning before everyone wakes up."

Molly did a big stretchy-yawn, then kicked off her duvet and said, "Alright, Stevie-pops, we're coming to get you!" Then she tiptoed over to the window, I think to check if it was snowing. It wasn't.

Molly had just wriggled into her astronaut costume, complete with space helmet, purple leg warmers and tutu, when Fenella suddenly bolted upright in bed, which was so alarming that both Molly and I yelped.

Fenella whipped her silky eye-mask off, blinked at the clock, then glared at us.

"What are you two up to? It's not even six in the morning!"

"We're going to look for Steve the shepherd," Molly said.

"What are you *really* doing?"

"We're going for a walk. Want to come?" I obviously did not want her to come, but I said it because, number one, I knew she wouldn't take me up on the offer and, number two, I had to cover up the fact that we actually were about to undertake an extensive manhunt across the Hampshire countryside for a holy shepherd.

Fenella flopped back onto her bed and pulled her eye-mask back on. "Not a chance. Now disappear, would you? People are trying to sleep around here."

"If anyone asks where we are, tell them we've not gone far and we'll be back soon."

"Whatever – now shush!"

I had meant to steal some more clothes from Dad for Balthazar, what with his clothes probably still being wet from the bath and also blatantly not of this time, but I didn't want to go in and wake Dad up, so I took some of Grandfather's clothes out of the tumble dryer downstairs.

When we got to the bathroom, Balthazar was lying on the floor, clutching his stomach and groaning.

"Is he alright?" I asked, pulling Molly in and closing the door behind us.

"I told him not to, but he wouldn't listen." The Angel Gabriel was sitting on the toilet lid, idly flicking through a very old copy of *House & Garden*.

"I was so hungry, see, and it all smelled so...enticing," Balthazar groaned.

"What's he talking about?" Molly asked.

"Hunger, the ultimate mortal weakness," the Angel Gabriel said.

Oops! I'd forgotten to feed the wise man. Bit of an oversight. "What did he eat?"

Balthazar pointed a quivering finger towards a basket of dusty and very old potpourri and then towards what looked like an equally ancient and now emptied tube of toothpaste.

"I think you'll be okay," I said and pulled him up from the floor. "I'll get you an egg butty when we're out to make up for it."

"Your pops are going to smell tremendous!" Molly said, then clapped her hands in delight.

"Here, put these on," I said, handing Balthazar a pair of Grandfather's raspberry-coloured corduroy trousers and what I then realized was Grandmother's flowery jumper.

He checked himself out in the mirror. "Not bad, not bad at all."

Then he groaned, bent over and, as Molly had predicted, did a very pleasingly scented apricotty fart.

It was still dark as we crept out the back door, through the garden and around to the stable block.

"Are you sure there are no camels or horses available?" Balthazar asked. "It's just a donkey is a little below my station."

"If it is good enough for Mary, mother of Our Lord, it is good enough for you," the Angel Gabriel told him.

"He's probably right," I said, "but we're not going by donkey."

"We're not?" Molly said, looking very upset.

"No, we're going by ride-on lawnmower."

That cheered her up a bit.

"A what?" the Angel Gabriel and Balthazar said at the same time.

I gestured at the lawnmower, which they were both, in fact, leaning on. "It's meant for cutting the grass, but I see no reason why it can't be transportation too."

They both jumped up and looked at the lawnmower like it was the strangest thing in the world.

"This metal beast can move?" Balthazar said.

"Sure, you just have to start the ignition and off it goes," I said, hoping that was true.

"You know how to ride one of these contraptions?" the Angel Gabriel asked.

"Sure," I said again. "Theoretically."

I had never actually driven one, but, really, how hard could it be? It's like Grandfather told me that time in the Landy: *just point the thing in the right direction, it'll do*

the rest. Now, I know commandeering garden machinery in normal circumstances might get my name struck off the *nice* list for being both dangerous and, let's face it, *naughty*, but I figured as I was saving Christmas I might get a pass.

Molly and I squashed into the driver's seat and the Angel Gabriel and Balthazar climbed into the little trailer – which Geoffrey uses for moving logs – that I'd hitched on to the back.

I turned the key in the ignition and the lawnmower spluttered into life. I put my foot down on the *GO!* pedal and, very happily, off we went. I say happily – Balthazar let out a little terror-scream and the Angel Gabriel covered his eyes, but I think they were enjoying themselves really.

I was a little wibbly-wobbly with the steering to start with and I fell off and had to run and jump back on, which caused an awful lot of fuss from my new biblical friends. But once I'd got the hang of it, we were chugging off to the back fields in no time. Without wanting to sound big-headed, I was a ride-on-lawnmower-driving natural!

Once I'd expertly manoeuvred us through the gate,

I pushed my foot down for a little more gas and we lurched forward at what felt like breakneck speed, but in reality was probably not all that much faster than a gentle jogging pace.

"This is a doddle! Nothing is going to stop us from finding Steve at this pace!" I shouted back at the others.

And I really thought that.

But I didn't count on Grandma the turkey leaping out from the darkness and straight into our path.

I'll never forget the look of steely determination in that bird's eyes.

I've thought about it a lot since, and I know people don't think turkeys are that clever, but there was something about that surprise attack which made me think she knew exactly what she was doing.

Think about it...Operation Save Christmas...

Not the best time of year for Grandma Turkey. She probably wouldn't be completely behind our mission, for obvious reasons.

Anyway, there was a BUMP.

A SQUAWK!

A yell of "NOOOOOO!" from Molly.

A shower of feathers.

Then finally another scream from Molly of, "OSCAR! You've run over Grandma!" like it was somehow my fault.

I turned off the ignition and we all climbed off the mower. The Angel Gabriel took his flat cap off to provide some light from his halo and we stood around the motionless body of Grandma.

"Oh dear," Balthazar said.

"Oh well," said the Angel Gabriel.

"Minute's silence?" I suggested.

Molly got down on her knees next to Grandma and flipped up her astronaut's helmet. "Is she dead? Like, Harold-dead?"

I was about to say, "Yes, I'm afraid so," but Grandma opened one beady eye and looked straight at me in a way that made me think she was more than a bit annoyed. Which, considering she was the one who launched herself at me, seemed a little unjustified.

Molly was pleased though. She said, "She's alive!" then leaped up and did a little celebratory turkey dance, which involved a lot of enthusiastic head-jutting and *gobble-gobble*-ing.

Grandma staggered to her feet. She looked okay, apart from the fact that one of her legs wasn't quite working properly. I did feel bad about that. Even if it wasn't strictly my fault.

"We have to take her back to the stables and look after her until she's better," Molly announced. But then she slapped her hand to her helmet and said, "But we can't because human Grandmother will want to stick a lemon up her bum and eat her for Christmas."

"Maybe we should just leave her here then?" I suggested.

"No!" Molly said and stomped her foot. "She'll get eaten by badgers."

"I don't think badgers eat turkeys, Molls," I said.

"It will be the wolves that get her," Balthazar said, which was unhelpful.

So I said, "We don't really have wolves, it's more likely to be foxes." Which I realized, when I saw the look of dread on Molly's face, was also unhelpful.

"Well, I won't let her be eaten by badgers or wolves or foxes or Grandmother!" Molly said, then she started crying. "Osky, you have to help her. You did run her over with the ride-on lawnmower, after all."

So because I was feeling guilty about the turkey-based traffic collision and I don't like seeing Molly cry and I didn't want to be responsible for a turkey being savaged to death by any countryside animal, I went against my better judgement and said, "Okay, Molly, I think I have an idea."

17

Glad tidings of great joy

– although none to report at this time

I'd decided the best course of action was to take Grandma the turkey with us and then put her in the downstairs bathroom with the others until her leg was better or I could find a place that would take her in. An animal sanctuary or something. I had thought about calling George Budwell to come and collect her, but Molly wouldn't have that. She shook her head so violently that her space helmet flew off, and said, "He'll only give Grandma to some other family who'll stick a lemon up her bum and eat her," which was probably true.

We positioned ourselves around Grandma and I gave

the instructions. "Okay, on three, everybody grab a corner and lift."

"Do turkeys have corners?" the Angel Gabriel asked.

"Just get a hold of her and lift on three," I said and then I counted down.

On one, we all lifted, although I felt like I was taking most – if not all – of Grandma's weight.

Carefully, and with Balthazar repeating, "Oh my goodness, oh my goodness, oh my goodness, I'm touching it!" and the Angel Gabriel making an "*Ewwwwwwwwww*" noise, we carried Grandma and put her in the trailer.

Neither Balthazar nor the Angel Gabriel had been one hundred per cent delighted about the idea of sharing their temporary lodgings with injured poultry, but I promised them that it wouldn't be for long. We'd locate Steve and track down Mary and Joseph and get them all back to where they should be in no time.

Probably.

Hopefully.

I mean, I still hadn't the first idea about where to even start looking for Mary and Joseph, so there were *some* lingering doubts.

So off we went, with Molly singing a "Get better soon,

Grandma Turkey" song which she made up on the spot and the Angel Gabriel and Balthazar squealing every time Grandma moved closer to them.

I stopped smack-bang in the middle of the first sheep field and killed the ignition. Then I cupped my hands around my mouth and shouted, "Steve! Shepherd Steve, are you out there? You okay, Steve? We have come to deliver you back to Bethlehem!"

"Er, excuse me? Did *you* just announce our arrival?" The Angel Gabriel did not look that happy. "Because if I remember correctly, it is *I* who does the announcing, understand?"

"Because that went so well for you last time..." I muttered very quietly under my breath.

But angels must have super-hearing or something, because he said, "You'd do well to remember that when this is over, I'll have my smiting powers back."

"You going to threaten me with fire and brimstone again? Because I checked, and that wasn't you, that was God."

Ha. Had him there.

"Let's just look for Steve," the Angel Gabriel said, trying to sound a bit superior.

"I'll have you know that's what I'm doing right now, with my eyeballs!" I said, trying to sound a bit superior too.

"Are you looking with your very biggest eyeballs though, Osky?" Molly asked. "Because I can't see a shepherd anywhere. Even if I stretch my eyelids really wide."

"She's right," Balthazar said, "he's not here."

"Everybody back on the mower then," I said and restarted the engine. "Let's go on to the next field."

"Okay, but so everybody's clear and to avoid any awkward situations like the one we just experienced, I shall be the one to announce our arrival next time," the Angel Gabriel said.

"Er, why?" I asked.

"Because you made a complete mess of it. I usually start with something positive, you know, to get people on side. Let me see...usually I'd lead in with something like, 'Fear not, glad tidings of great joy I bring, to you and all mankind.' And besides, *I'm* the professional."

I looked at him, frankly incredulous. "You do remember how we ended up in this situation in the first place?"

He stuck his nose in the air, like he did not appreciate being reminded, and said, "Drive on!" quite snappily.

We drove around for about two hours, stopping in field after field and listening to the Angel Gabriel announcing our arrival with great joy (although sounding increasingly frustrated) to yet another disinterested-looking flock of sheep. And one time to a slightly too interested-looking bull, who was watching us from behind a fence. But never a shepherd.

It was starting to get light and Molly was complaining about her tummy rumbling. I couldn't blame her; I was hungry too. I checked my watch.

"Argh! We'll need to get back soon, before people notice how long we've been gone and send out a search party. We'll have to find Steve later. Maybe we can try the fields over the other side of the village. And I'll see if I can find out any more information on whether this sheep poacher has been seen again."

"Oh bums," Molly said. "I really wanted to catch that shepherd."

"It is most disappointing," the Angel Gabriel said.

It was. To be honest, it felt like a disaster. A whole morning searching and we hadn't had a whiff of a shepherd. Donald the donkey and Balthazar had been easy finds. Steve was proving a little more tricky, and the countdown to Christmas was well and truly on. The others knew it too.

"Are you absolutely sure we need them all? Like, if we don't find Steve, could we just move on to Mary and Joseph?" I asked as we clambered back onto the mower.

The Angel Gabriel shook his head. "All must return. They all have their roles to play."

"Okay, well don't worry, today is only the twenty-second of December so we still have three days to do this. That's loads of time." It absolutely was *not* loads of time. I said that not because I wasn't worried, but because the mood in the ride-on lawnmower was a bit flat. I felt like somebody should try and raise our spirits. Which some might argue should be the job of an angel, but he looked more miserable than anybody.

At least Grandma looked like she'd enjoyed herself. Every time I'd started the engine she'd stuck her head right up and made very soft *gobble-gobble* noises. I swear I spotted a smile on her face when the wind ruffled through her feathers as we headed down the hill towards home.

When we reached the back gate of Barlington Hall, it

202

was just coming up to nine in the morning. As we weren't having a family breakfast, I didn't think anyone would have missed us just yet. We parked the lawnmower in the stable block, then we all grabbed a turkey corner again and struggled across the lawn, into the house and down the corridor to the bathroom hideout.

While the Angel Gabriel and Balthazar stood with their backs pressed against the wall, whimpering every time Grandma strutted near one of them, I dashed to the kitchen to get some turkey feed and a bowl for water.

I wasn't a hundred per cent certain what turkeys eat, but I reckoned a box of Grandmother's luxury muesli and a box full of porridge oats would probably do the job for the time being. I skittered out of the kitchen and round the corner, just avoiding Grandmother, who was in the hall, giving Margaret instructions about the soon-to-start rehearsal.

Back in the bathroom, I put the plug in the bath and tipped in the oats and muesli. I filled the bowl from the tap so Grandma had something to drink, and then I pointed to the little bin in the corner and gave Grandma a strong look. "If you need to go to the loo, you go in there, okay?"

Grandma Turkey didn't reply, because she was too busy stuffing her face with a Swiss and Scottish luxury breakfast.

"So he remembers to feed the turkey," Balthazar said pointedly.

I gestured at the bathtub. "Do help yourself." He looked horrified. I smiled. "Don't worry, I didn't forget you. Here." I handed him a banana and a wedge of Mum's Christmas cake. "That should fill you up."

He took a bite. Chewed for a very long time. Gulped. Then said, "Unusual but not unpleasant."

Molly and I snuck back into the main part of the house and bumped into Grandfather in the entrance hall.

"Good morning, you two! How are you on this bright and blessed day?" he said. "Are you ready for rehearsals? I hope you're energized and raring to go!"

I wasn't energized or raring to go. I was really quite tired from all the turkey-wrangling and shepherd-hunting, but I said, "Absolutely!"

Down the corridor, Grandmother poked her head out of the drawing room and clapped her hands. "Do hurry up, we are pressed for time as it is and there is much to be done!"

She was right about that. I had:

- To find Mary and Joseph and a shepherd named Steve
- A turkey to rehome
- An angel and a wise man to keep hidden
- And most unimportantly (not that I'd say that to Grandmother), a nativity play to rehearse

I was starting to wonder if it all could be done, and I felt panic bubbling away in my stomach. It was too much for one boy to cope with. I couldn't do all those things! I'd fail and then Mary and Joseph wouldn't make it back to Bethlehem and there'd be no Christmas and no presents, *and* Mum and Dad wouldn't meet – because why would he be dressed as an elf and carolling on Christmas Day if there was no Christmas Day? And then there'd be no me and I wouldn't get to do all the things I was supposed to do. And there might be no Jesus either and, from what I could remember from RE lessons, he had a bit to be getting on with as well. And also I wouldn't be able to ask the Angel Gabriel the favour I wanted to ask him and—

"Oscar," Grandfather said, looking at me kindly. "Are you okay? You have gone quite pale."

"I...I...it's just the shepherd and the play and Grandma...it's all too much!" I blurted out.

Grandfather put his hand on my shoulder. "I understand – performance anxiety. Listen, if you don't want to do it, you don't have to."

We were talking about different things, but even so, when he said that, I knew giving up wasn't an option. I shook my head. "No, it's fine. I can do it. I have to."

"Well, I for one have absolute faith in you, young Oscar," Grandfather said, and he looked me in the eye in a way that made me know he really did. "I can tell you are the type of person who can achieve anything if they put their mind to it."

Sure, he didn't know what I was up against, but just him telling me that he believed in me made me think that I might actually stand a chance of saving Christmas and stopping all the doom the Angel Gabriel kept banging on about. Operation Save Christmas was all systems go.

18

Away in a
sheepies' field

All of Margaret's pastries had already been eaten, so Molly and I grabbed a couple of our magnificent mince pies from the kitchen – not exactly breakfast food, but there are different rules around eating during the Christmas holidays – then made our way to the drawing room. All the family were there, waiting to rehearse. Aunty Camilla was lying on the sofa, rubbing her baby bump in circles – I'd be surprised if that baby didn't come out spinning. Uncle Patryk was sitting beside her, quietly repeating his lines and looking thoughtful. Fenella and Hugo were sitting on footstools, showing off their very neat hair and very straight backs. I bet Aunty Marigold had never told either of them they have the posture of a prawn.

Uncle James and Aunty Marigold were on the sofa next to Mum, who looked like she wanted to be anywhere else. Dad was in an armchair, looking through his script, and Geoffrey the gardener and Margaret were loitering at the back of the room, looking slightly anxious – until Grandfather told them to sit on a sofa, and that anyone who was in the Cuthbert-Anderson nativity was officially part of the family.

"I say," Grandfather said as Geoffrey and Margaret sat down. "I don't suppose either of you have seen anything of that turkey young Molly took a shine to?"

Molly and I gave each other a wide-eyed look.

"Not a feather," Geoffrey said, which was a relief. "Probably escaped out of the stable and long gone."

I struggled to pay attention to much of the rehearsal because I kept thinking about all the other stuff I had to do – like finding that shepherd and quick. I considered if it would be possible to construct some kind of shepherd-trap, but I couldn't really think what to use as bait. Or, in fact, how to build it. Or where to even put it. So it was a bit of a rubbish idea.

Luckily, it didn't matter that I was paying zero interest to the rehearsal, because we never got to my part.

Grandmother has very high standards. Fenella and Hugo obviously said their lines perfectly. Dad spoke too fast and was a "trifle too monotone" in his delivery. Margaret was too quiet. Molly added her own special spin. She said, "And so Mary and Joseph travelled to Bethlehem because if they didn't the angels would smite them with hailstones."

Grandmother said, "Gracious, Molly, an angel wouldn't say that!"

Molly said, "That's *exactly* what an angel would say if he wanted his own way," which was true, but there was no point telling Grandmother that.

Aunty Camilla, despite being nine months pregnant, wasn't doing a very good job of acting like a pregnant lady apparently.

"I just don't think the Blessed Virgin Mary, the mother of Jesus Christ Our Lord, would waddle with quite so little grace, Camilla," Grandmother said, a look of displeasure creasing her face as she watched Aunty Camilla walking across the room with Uncle Patryk, who was actually doing a very convincing job of pretending to lead an invisible donkey.

Aunty Camilla didn't seem happy about being told she waddled without grace, but I could see Dad and Uncle James giggling behind their scripts.

"Mummy, I can't see my feet, I can't really fit behind the steering wheel of a car, but one

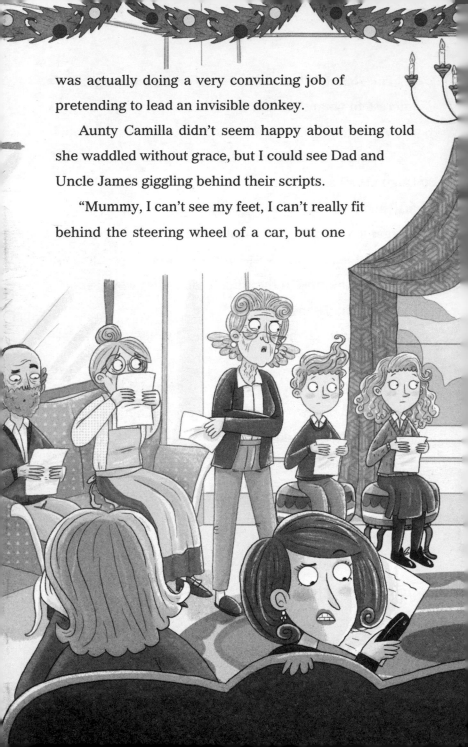

thing I *can* do at the moment is act exactly like a pregnant woman!"

"A pregnant woman, yes. But the sacred vessel of our Lord? I think that requires you to dig a little deeper, darling."

"Deeper? How do I do deeper?" Aunty Camilla snapped.

Before Grandmother could answer, Patryk said, "Perhaps I could demonstrate?"

Patryk then did the best impression of Mary I have ever seen. If it was grace Grandmother wanted, Patryk was doing it.

I think everyone was a little stunned, but mainly Grandmother.

"How? How did you do that?" she said, wafting her script around.

"I acted a little, when I was younger," Patryk explained.

"Read your lines," she demanded, as if asking for proof.

Patryk took Aunty Camilla's hand, looked into her eyes and said, "Do not worry, my love. Though the road may be long, I am here with you, every step of the way."

He was amazing! I think even Aunty Camilla had a tear in her eye, which she wiped away, saying something about pregnancy hormones.

Molly stood up and started clapping and said, "Uncle Patryk, take a bow! You're the best actor I have ever seen ever!" which made Grandmother flinch.

"Wonderful, Patryk!" Grandfather said. "What a thing! A real actor in the family."

Grandmother made this sharp coughing noise.

"*Another* real actor," Grandfather corrected himself. "Wasn't he good, Minty?"

"Yes, he was," Grandmother admitted. "Everyone, take note of how Patryk put real emotion into his performance. Camilla, you've seen how it should be done. Perhaps when you are atop of the donkey it will help you bring some more elegance and authenticity to the role."

"The donkey? *What* donkey?" Aunty Camilla yelped.

The rehearsal kind of came to a stop then while Grandmother explained about Donald. I don't think Aunty Camilla was very pleased about riding a donkey into church and we left them to what Grandfather called a "heated discussion", but looked more like a full-blown row to me.

I gave Molly a piggyback ride down the corridor and, thinking we were alone, I said, "Let's get the others and go find that shepherd!"

"What shepherd?" came two voices behind us.

I swung round to see Fenella and Hugo, their arms crossed and identical hard looks on their faces.

"Erm...the shepherd inside me...the one that I'm trying to tap into for the performance," I said, a little uncertainly.

"What others? What are you two up to?" Fenella continued.

"Nothing," I said, trying to arrange my face to look as innocent as possible.

"Hmmmmm," Hugo hmmmmed. "We're watching you. Fenella told me about your early-morning walk and we think you're up to something. Don't we, Nellers?"

"We do. Don't we, Hugo?"

"Yes, we do, I *literally* just said that."

"Watch all you like," I said and then I just stood there, letting them watch us. For quite some time. While we did nothing. But stand there. Being watched.

Eventually, they either got bored or felt too awkward or realized it had got a bit weird, because they both huffed at the exact same time, then spun on their heels and waltzed off down the corridor, Hugo's quiff and Fenella's ringlets bouncing in time.

"If you're up to something, we'll find out," Fenella called over her shoulder in an airy yet still somehow very menacing tone.

That was all I needed, those two on my case. As if things weren't stressful enough! But with them gone, for the moment at least, I had a chance to do some investigating into our missing shepherd. I figured that Geoffrey, the gardener, might be the person to ask about this "sheep poacher". So I piggybacked Molly out to the front garden to have a word with him.

"Still at large, I believe," Geoffrey said, turning off the leaf blower. "Last I heard, someone had been spotted in the fields at the back of Mrs Tadworth's cottage, but could have just been a rambler. Why are you so interested anyway?"

"No reason," I said. It might have just been a rambler, but, with no other clues, it was the best chance we had.

"We're not up to anything," Molly said out of nowhere, which made it sound like we were *definitely* up to something.

"Hmmmm," Geoffrey said, so we quickly left him to his leaf-blowing and headed back inside. It was time to go and find out how things were in the bathroom.

As soon as I opened the door, two things instantly became clear:

Grandma Turkey had not listened to a word I said about using the bin if she had some business to do.

The Angel Gabriel and Balthazar were not huge fans of turkeys. I pulled the shower curtain back and found them cowering in the muesli-filled bath while Grandma strutted about the room like she owned the place.

"Come on," I said. "We're heading out for Steve again. There was a sighting, near the Tadworths' place, not too far from here, which is good because I don't think we can risk another ride on the mower in the daylight."

They sidled past Grandma Turkey and we snuck down the corridor and out the back door.

Soon, an angel (who was still making a lot of fuss about the chaffage from his Just Jeans), a wise man, an astronaut in a tutu and I were trudging up the hill round the back of Mrs Tadworth's, hoping that no one would notice us.

"I think we're going to find Steve," Molly announced. "It feels like a Steve-finding kind of day, don't you think?"

"I sure hope so, Molls," I said, but from the top of the hill I could see so much countryside spreading out

216

around us, I felt our chances of stumbling across a holy shepherd were fading.

We stopped to take in the view for a moment and get our breath back.

"Just think, Mary and Joseph and a shepherd named Steve are out there somewhere," Molly said.

Balthazar shook his head. "But how ever are we going to find them?"

Looking across at field after field, it did suddenly seem like we were on an impossible mission, and my heart felt heavy. Sure, Christmas isn't always perfect. Families argue and people eat too much and sometimes they get disappointed when they ask for a computer game and get another set of pyjamas, but I think it's what's under all that that counts. Just being together and celebrating a magical time of the year when us kids can believe in the impossible is what it's really about. And as Molly would say, the feeling that you get when you go to bed on Christmas Eve...well, that's really quite majestiful.

Christmas was something worth saving.

And so was I. I just had to believe in the impossible too.

"I know!" Molly shouted. "I'll ask those sheep

snuggled together over by that tree if they've seen anything." And off she marched towards them.

While Molly went off to not talk to sheep, the Angel Gabriel, Balthazar and I continued to scan the fields around us. There was so much land. It all felt a bit hopeless. There was no sign of Steve anywhere.

But then Molly shouted, "Well, that's a bit rude!"

"What's that, Molls?" I called over.

"This sheep is a bit rude," she said, pointing to one. "I think there's something wrong with it."

I started walking over. "Molls, we don't really have time for this."

"It told me to go away! That's rude!"

"Molly." I flipped up her astronaut helmet and said as kindly as I could, "You can't really talk to animals."

"Well, I don't want to talk to this one any more because it's a great big fluffy-meany-pants."

I was a little puzzled as to why Molly had taken against that particular sheep so much. It looked like a pretty standard sheep to me.

"All I did was ask about Steve!"

"Go away!"

"*See?* Rude!"

218

I paused. I frowned. Had it...? No – that would be mad... I shook my head. It couldn't have spoken. Sheep don't speak. They certainly don't tell people to go away.

"Leave me be."

"Say please!" Molly said.

"WHAAAAAA!" I shouted, because what else do you shout when you hear a sheep talk?

Anyway, my *WHAAAAA!* spooked the sheep and it darted off to the back of the huddle, revealing a man, who was curled up in a tight ball behind it.

"Look!" Molly shouted. "There was a man hiding behind that talking sheep!"

The man was wearing very muddy clothes, sandals and, he looked quite, well, shepherdy.

"Steve?" I said. "Steve…is that you?"

Steve didn't answer.

I crouched down. "Are you okay?"

Steve still didn't answer, but started rocking backwards and forwards, which made me think that perhaps the answer to that question was no.

Balthazar and the Angel Gabriel appeared by my side.

"Ah, it is Steve the Shepherd, what wondrous news! It is I, the Angel Gabriel!" the Angel Gabriel boomed.

Steve yelped and scurried backwards. "Leave me be! Leave me be!"

"Steve's scared," Molly said.

Steve looked Molly up and down and then said, in a voice that was mostly breath, "What *are* you?"

"Today I am a ballerina-ing astronaut," she said.

"That's Molly, my sister," I explained.

"Don't worry, Steve," Balthazar said brightly. "We're here to help."

"You must come with us. You have a very important job to do!" the Angel Gabriel said.

"That's what you said last time and I ended up here!"

And then, before anyone could stop him, Steve was

up and running, his dirty clothes and beard streaming out behind him.

He couldn't just sit there and watch and wait and stay seated like shepherds are supposed to, could he? Why did saving Christmas have to be quite so difficult?

19

While shepherds watched their flocks by night

there may have also been some cuddling going on

I don't think any of us had thought Steve would do a runner, so we stood there, probably for too long, as he sprinted off at a surprisingly speedy rate considering the terrain and his footwear.

"Someone probably ought to go after him," Balthazar said.

"Yes, probably," the Angel Gabriel said. We all looked at each other and then took off across the field.

Molly quickly got left behind, so Balthazar scooped her up under his arm, which basically meant it was down to me or the Angel Gabriel to catch up with Steve.

"You...have to...stop!" I shouted, between gasps. "Or...everything will be...doomed!"

"DoOoOOOooMed!" Molly repeated in a bit of a wobbly voice because of all the bouncing up and down under Balthazar's arm.

"Do something!" I shouted at the Angel Gabriel. "He's getting away!"

The Angel Gabriel shouted, "Steve the Shepherd, I command you to stop!"

But that didn't work – if anything, Steve got faster.

"Stop or...he'll rain fire...and brimstones...down on you!" I added. "And he's got...some other angel mates...with boulders and worms...that he'll set on you too!"

That didn't work either. Steve looked over his shoulder and shouted, "You'll never catch me!"

But we did. Mere seconds after he said that. Because what actually comes before a fall is a very disinterested-looking sheep.

Steve was so busy looking at us and not at the sheep, which had idly wandered into his path, that he flipped right over the thing. It was gymnastically very good. I'd give him a ten for all the somersaulting in the air, but only a three for the landing, as it wasn't very graceful and he made a big *UFFFFF!* sound.

We stood over him as he clutched his side, groaning. "Why are the sheep here so well built?" He struggled to his feet and looked at the slowly retreating sheep with an expression somewhere between awe and dismay. "They're just so sturdy. The ones at home are scrawny in comparison."

"That's because you have been transported two thousand years into the future," Balthazar said. "Things are a little different here. Do remind me to tell you all about just lavender bubble bath, it is sensationally good."

"I…I…I'm where?" Steve stammered.

"Other sheepies Field. Top of the hill. Near Mrs Tadworth's cottage. Chipping Bottom. Hampshire. England. The British Isles. The United Kingdom. The world," Molly said, quite triumphantly.

"The thing is," I said, "the Angel Gabriel here went *all out*, shall we say, in the power department when he came down to Earth back in zero BC – that's the time you're from – when he was announcing the birth of the baby Jesus to you. But he accidentally shot you and Balthazar and Mary and Joseph and a donkey called Donald through time and space to here, Chipping Bottom."

"I don't know these people. But I do remember a flash of light," Steve said, touching the side of his head and closing his eyes. "Yes, I was in my field."

"Watching your flocks? Seated on the ground?" I said.

"Yes! How did you know?"

"Call it a lucky hunch."

"There was the flash of light, as I said. Then a voice…"

"A boomy voice?" Molly said.

"Yes, it was rather."

"I think you mean impressive," the Angel Gabriel said.

"It said, 'A baby will be…oh…oh…uh-oh…too much…no… oh NOOOOOOOO!' And then there was a big bang and then I woke up here, in this field of pleasingly woolly sheep." He looked at them admiringly. "They have been a great comfort."

"Really?" I said.

"At night," he whispered, "when it grows dark and cold, I cuddle them."

"Okaaayyyy. Moving on. Fact is, Steve, we need to get you and Balthazar and Mary and Joseph back to

Bethlehem, or things aren't going to work out brilliantly for anybody and especially me."

"Who needs to be where?"

"You! And Balthazar, one of the wise men, and Mary and Joseph," Molly said.

"Wait...I met a Mary and Joseph yesterday."

"WHAT? WHEN? WHERE?" The Angel Gabriel grabbed Steve's arms and gave him a shake. "Tell us, tell us now! I command it!"

"When I say 'met', I mean I saw them from where I was sitting inside my sheep huddle."

"How did you know it was them?" I asked.

"Because they called each other Mary and Joseph. Why are they so important? What's going on? I'm so confused. Can I go back and cuddle my sheep?"

"No, you can't go and cuddle your sheep," I said.

"Ah, yes," the Angel Gabriel said, "I didn't quite get to the end of my announcement. Mary is with child. The son of God is going to be born in a stable in Bethlehem."

"Whaaaaaaaat?" Steve said. "The son of God?"

"Yup, the actual son of actual God," Molly said.

"And this Joseph, he's alright with all this, is he?" Steve asked.

"He's ecstatic, his child is going to be the Messiah!" The Angel Gabriel clapped his hands together.

"What's a Messiah?" Molly asked, which I was kind of glad about, because I'd been wondering the same thing.

"The chosen one, who is going to do God's will on Earth," the Angel Gabriel explained, before turning back to Steve. "And when I came down from the Realm of Glory to proclaim Jesus's birth, I was there to invite you to attend said birth."

"Inviting me to attend a *birth*? But why?"

"I don't mean you need to be there for the actual birthing – just pop your head into the lowly cattle shed afterwards and give your best wishes, drop off your gift, that sort of thing."

"No, I meant but why *me*?"

"Because Jesus is for everyone." The Angel Gabriel raised his arms. "The poor, the meek *and* the lowly, not just wealthy wise men like our friend Balthazar here."

"Oi! Are you calling me poor and meek and lowly?" Steve said.

"Do you spend your nights in fields cuddling sheep?" the Angel Gabriel said.

Steve shrugged. "It's part of the job! But, point taken. And all the same, I might give it a miss."

"You can't! You have a very important role!"

"A very important role, hey?" Steve's chest puffed up.

"Essential," I said. "So essential that the whole thing can't happen without you."

"Essential, you say?"

"Yes, you are to act as a physical metaphor for Jesus's role on Earth, I think. At least I think that's what my teacher said."

"A physical metaphor? I don't know what one of those is, but if I'm *essential*, count me in! Oh! You mentioned a gift! What shall I get him? Is there a list?"

"Gifts are tricky." Balthazar nodded sagely. "But as you are a shepherd, and poor as you are, why not give him...I don't know...a lamb, maybe?"

"Or..." Steve beamed. "Maybe one of these super-woolly sheep!"

"I'd give him a pirate-racoon puppet," Molly said.

"Nobody will be giving any presents if we don't find Mary and Joseph soon – after today, there's only two days left to save Christmas!" I said. "Which way did they go? Did you hear anything?"

"They went that way." Steve pointed down to the village. "They were talking about making their way to Bethlehem on foot."

"*Bethlehem on foot?*" I said. "That's quite ambitious."

"They spoke about having got directions from that place yonder." He gestured at the village post office.

"They got directions to Bethlehem from the post office? How could anyone direct them all the way there… unless…" A thought struck me. "Hmmm, it is definitely possible, but I'd have to check."

"What is it, Osky? Your forehead has gone all crinkly-crunkly," Molly said.

"I was thinking, remember how we almost drove to Hampshire County in America. What if there is another Bethlehem in England? They might be trying to go there by mistake."

"Another Bethlehem? No WAY!" Molly said.

"It's a possibility. Let's go to the post office and ask." I began to walk down the hill and then stopped, slapping my hand to my forehead. "Oh bums! It's Sunday, it won't be open. We can't go until tomorrow."

I suddenly felt irrationally angry at my parents for not going back to get my phone after they'd forgotten to remind me to bring it. If I had it, I would have been able to check there and then.

"Okay, don't panic," I said. "We'll head back to the house and I'll do some internet investigation to find out if there are any other Bethlehems. I think I remember seeing a computer – of sorts – in the library. Steve, you're coming with us. Now, tell me, how do you feel about turkeys?"

20

Away in a manger,

no church for our play

It took a little while to persuade Steve to leave the sheep behind in the field. He said it went against the fibre of his very being to leave a flock untended. I tried to reassure him that they'd be safe – that there were no lions or bears in Chipping Bottom – but then Molly went and put the frighteners on him by talking about savage badgers.

Anyway, eventually we talked him down from the hillside and we trundled back across the fields to Barlington Hall.

Annoyingly, Geoffrey was working in the garden,

which made sneaking back into the downstairs bathroom hideout a little more tricky.

Molly said, "I'll handle this, Osky." She skipped up to Geoffrey and forced him to watch a very loud and shouty performance of "Little Donkey", complete with wonky cartwheels and cancan kicks. It was an ace distraction and we managed to get in unnoticed.

With me, Molly, the Angel Gabriel, Balthazar, Steve and Grandma all in the bathroom, it quickly became clear that we were most definitely at least one turkey too many. I really needed to find a place to take her that wouldn't end up with her getting a lemon stuck up her bum, and soon.

I thought Grandma Turkey might kick off at having to share the place with another new person, but actually she seemed rather taken with Steve.

Molly *gobble-gobble*d at her and said, "Right, Steve, I've introduced you to Grandma."

Steve pressed his hands together, looked Grandma in the eyes and said, "Hello, Grandma, what a wondrous creature you are." Then he sat down on the floor cross-legged and she strutted over to him, plonked herself down and put her head on his knee. I suppose shepherding and turkey-herding involve a similar skill set.

Molly and I did a few supply runs to the kitchen so Balthazar and Steve had something to eat. I've never seen two people smash through a forty-eight pack of Jaffa Cakes so quickly.

"What are these indescribable delights?" Balthazar said, holding one up to examine it. "Is it a biscuit or a cake?"

"That," I said, "is one of the biggest mysteries of the modern world."

"I got you these too," Molly said, proudly handing over the three enthusiastically-piped home-made Christmas tree biscuits that she'd made with Mum. "Look, it's an angel and a wise man and a shepherd."

"Is that supposed to be *me*?" the Angel Gabriel said, clearly unimpressed, but I shot him a dark look and he said, "Magnificent!" which made Molly beam.

I'd also managed to swipe some more of Dad's clothes for Steve, so he looked less like a shepherd and really quite Christmassy in his knitted Christmas pudding jumper.

Molly and I then had to dash to the dining room for

a family lunch. It was shepherd's pie and Molly would only eat it once I'd convinced her that there were no actual shepherds like Steve, minced up under the potato. After we'd finished, we snuck back to check in with the Angel Gabriel and Balthazar and interrupted them in the middle of a game of I spy.

"Looks like you're managing to keep yourselves amused. But I brought you these in case you got bored," I said and handed the Angel Gabriel a pack of Uno cards.

I thought if they were busy they'd be less likely to get into any mischief. I'd then be able to get on with my investigation into locating Mary and Joseph and formulating a plan as to how to get them back without worrying.

Once I was certain they were all settled and I had clarified the rules of Uno for the thirty-hundredth time, I gave them all, including Grandma, a stern look and said, "We'll be back later with news. Until then, stay here and stay hidden. I'm going to think of a plan for that turkey and find out what I can about Mary and Joseph's movements. Hopefully they haven't gone far. Tomorrow is Christmas Eve's eve – we don't have much time."

We met everyone in the drawing room for the final rehearsal of the day. Mum, Dad, my aunties and uncles and Grandfather were all busy cutting out paper snowflakes and stars to decorate the church. Mum gave me a little wave as we crept in. I sat next to the fire and Molly sat down by Mum's feet. Fenella was busy performing. She was mid-flow, Grandmother nodding encouragingly as she delivered her lines.

"Superb," Grandmother said once she had finished. "Molly, Oscar Charles, I do hope you took note of Fenella's excellent diction."

Hugo was up next. He made a few grumbles about being an angel, but Grandmother shut that down pretty quickly. I reckon that if he didn't want to be an angel, he probably shouldn't have made such a good job of his performance, because Grandmother told him he was wholly convincing and congratulated herself on her casting decisions.

"Your turn now," Grandmother said, gesturing at me to get up.

Mum and Dad stopped cutting. Mum gave me a smile and Dad did a double thumbs up.

I felt a bit nervous, to be honest, with everything going on, I hadn't had much chance to even think about my lines. But if I was going to be in the family nativity, I wanted to do it properly. I guess it didn't help that Fenella and Hugo had been so good.

"I'll lead you in," Grandmother said. "You'll hear the end of 'While Shepherds Watched Their Flocks' and then an awe-inspiring vision will appear unto you – that will be me. Ready?"

I went to say yes, but she had already launched into a *very* loud and operatic version of the shepherd song.

"All glory be to God on high,

And to the Earth be peace;

Goodwill henceforth from highest heaven

Begin and never ceasssssssssssssssssse!"

She held that last note for a really long time, then waited until we all realized we needed to clap. Once she'd accepted the applause, she sort of loomed towards me, which was completely daunting and I think the reason I said, "Why are you? And who are you here?"

Grandmother's face fell. "No, no, no! That's not right. Try again. And could you please refer to my stage directions? It clearly says you must cover your eyes and tremble as I approach."

"I think I can manage that," I said. Grandmother in full-on Angel Gabriel mode was quite tremble-worthy.

"Well, go on then," she said impatiently, "or do you need me to lead you in with the final verse again?"

No one needed to hear that more than once. "I think I'll be fine," I said. "Just commence your looming."

"*Looming?* The Angel Gabriel does not loom! What a suggestion!"

237

"He does like a foot spa though," Molly piped up.

Grandmother ignored that. "I shall approach you in a veil of heavenly wonder and you tremble and deliver your line."

I nodded and Grandmother stalked towards me, apparently in a veil of heavenly wonder, which still felt quite loomy to me. I trembled and said, "You are who? And here are you why?" I knew it didn't sound right as soon as I said it.

Grandmother looked upwards and muttered something to the ceiling about all good directors facing challenges to which they must rise.

Grandfather winked at me, rose up from his armchair in a shower of paper cuttings and said, "What say we take a break? Shall I see if I can conjure us up some hot chocolate?"

Everyone leaped from their seats when he said that – even Aunty Camilla, who wasn't the quickest at getting up out of a chair, was pretty speedy. This meant Grandmother had no choice but to go along with a break.

Dad ruffled my hair. "Don't worry, champ, you'll knock their socks off on the night!"

Mum gave me a kiss on the head. "I thought you were great."

Molly and I were heading back into the drawing room with bellies full of hot chocolate and marshmallows, just as the front doorbell rang. Margaret answered and Mrs Tadworth strode in. She was wearing a skirt, a Barbour jacket and her hair was even more voluminous than the last time I'd seen her.

"Ah, Mrs Tadworth, is Her Ladyship expecting you?"

"I'm afraid I'm bringing some rather distressing news with regards to the church."

Grandmother appeared from down the corridor. "Vivian, how wonderful that you should pay us a surprise visit." She was smiling but she didn't seem that pleased to see her.

"Araminta, dreadful news, I am desperately sorry to have to tell you this, but the church roof has finally fallen through – quite spectacularly, I'm afraid."

Grandmother clutched her hand to her chest. "But the nativity!"

"Yes, terrible shame, but I think the congregation shall have to go to St Augustus's in West Farthington this year."

"But they have their own nativity."

"Indeed, I know this is horrible for you, but we may have to cancel the Cuthbert-Anderson show this year."

"No...this can't be true! This year is incredibly important! I have acquired a donkey and everything!" Grandmother had gone as grey as her cashmere cardigan.

Before Mrs Tadworth had a chance to unpick that statement, Grandfather walked into the entrance hall. "Ah, Vivian! Season's greetings! I must say, Minty here is directing a real belter of a performance this time. I think it may be her best."

"Reginald, lovely to see you, but I'm afraid I have delivered some rather upsetting news with regards to this year's nativity production. I'll leave Araminta to explain, as I must be on my way. Toodle-pip!"

Mrs Tadworth disappeared out the door with a smile on her face, looking more than a bit pleased with herself.

"Minty, old girl, what's wrong?"

Grandmother swallowed hard. "The nativity – it's been cancelled."

"And she had a donkey and everything!" Molly added.

"Minty, how can this be true?" Grandfather said.

Grandmother had a very far-off look in her eyes. "The church roof, it finally fell through. Do you know, I think I might need to go for a little lie-down. I...I'm sorry, Reginald, I know how much this meant to you."

And then, very slowly, she made her way up the staircase, passing Uncle James, Hugo and Fenella on their way down.

"I say," Uncle James said, "is everything alright with Mummy? She looked terribly grim just now."

"She's just received some bad news, I'm afraid," Grandfather said solemnly.

"The nativity has been cancelled," I said.

"And she had a donkey and everything!" Molly said again.

Even though I knew it would mean I'd have more time to find Mary and Joseph, I felt quite upset, for Grandmother and for me. I'll admit, despite fluffing my words in rehearsal, I was looking forward to being part of our family tradition.

"Gracious," Uncle James said, turning back up the stairs. "I'll go after her. Mummy, Mummy, wait up!"

"Oh, Grandfather, I'm sorry," Fenella said. "I know it meant a lot to you too."

"I'm not worried about the nativity! I'm only worried about your grandmother."

"But we thought the nativity was important to you," Hugo said. "That's what Grandmother keeps saying."

Grandfather looked at each of us in turn. "Now, you must promise to keep this information entre nous, all of you."

Molly frowned. "Entre nooooo?"

"He means between us," Fenella explained.

"Our lips are sealed," I said. "Aren't they?"

"You can count on us, Grandfather," Hugo said, and although I wasn't a hundred per cent sure about that, Grandfather seemed to be reassured.

"I admit this only to you, my dearest of grandchildren. If pressed, be very certain that I will deny that these words ever passed my lips, and I will leave you to deal with the repercussions yourselves."

"What is it? Tell us!" I said.

He looked at me again, a twinkle dancing in his eyes. "I am not terribly enthusiastic about the nativity."

Fenella gasped. "But, Grandfather, Grandmother has

us all here to do this for you! I don't think any of us are terribly enthusiastic about the nativity. We could have gone skiing! We're only doing it because she says it means so much to you and because it might be your last—"

Fenella suddenly stopped talking, but we all knew she was going to say it might be Grandfather's last Christmas.

Luckily, before anything really could be said about that, Molly shattered the sudden awkward atmosphere by shouting, "But I love the nativity! I'm going to be an angel! Listen to how good I am!" She pushed her chin up high in the air and boomed, "I am an angel! Now bow down to me or I shall smite you, one and all!" which made Grandfather chortle.

Then he said, "Well, whatever the reason you came, I am certainly very glad you are all here."

"Oh, I'm so sorry!" Fenella said and I thought she might cry. "My stupid mouth! I didn't mean that, about the skiing. I'm glad to be here too, I was just surprised, that's all, I...I..."

Grandfather smiled kindly at her. "Think no more of it, Fenella. I know how you feel."

"But do you really not like the nativity, Grandfather?" I asked.

"I don't like prancing about in costume in front of the whole village, no."

"Why do you do it then?" I asked.

"Because it is important to your grandmother and what is important to your grandmother, I have learned, becomes important to me."

"So all of us are doing the nativity performance just to keep Grandmother happy?" Hugo said.

Grandfather raised one of his bushy eyebrows. "Would you like to see an unhappy Lady Cuthbert-Anderson?"

We all shook our heads quite fiercely. No one liked the thought of an unhappy Lady Cuthbert-Anderson.

"No, I didn't think so," Grandfather continued, "and so actors in the village nativity we shall be! This nativity will go ahead in one form or another, I shall see to that, you mark my words! Cuthbert-Andersons never surrender!"

I know we had slightly different aims – Grandfather wanted to save a pretend nativity and I wanted to save the real one – but while my mission was obviously way more important, his stirring speech gave me the belief that I stood a chance of doing it. I'd already found an angel, a donkey, a wise man and a shepherd. Now, I would hunt down Mary and Joseph and I'd return them all to their rightful place. Christmas was going to get saved, and even though there was only just over two days to go, I would be the kid to do it.

21

O' little town of Bethlehem

– is that the one in Wales or London?

Grandfather hurried off down the corridor and Molly and I were left with Fenella and Hugo in the entrance hall.

"What are you doing now?" Hugo asked.

The answer was that I was heading to the library to research Bethlehems and local turkey sanctuaries, but I did not tell him that. I said, "Nothing."

"Where were you earlier? We couldn't find you," Fenella said.

"Nowhere."

Her face grew all pinched-looking. "You must have been *somewhere*."

"We were around." I shrugged. "It's a big place."

Hugo narrowed his eyes. "Hmmm. We still think you're up to something, don't we, Nellers?"

"We do and we're going to find out what."

"Okay, good luck with that, because we're not up to anything, are we, Molly?"

Molly shook her head violently and said, "No! We're not up to anything, we're up to *something*!"

I looked at the ceiling and closed my eyes for a moment. She really was such a liability. "She doesn't know what she's talking about." I grabbed her hand and headed off to the library before Hugo and Fenella could grill us any more.

Molly kept watch at the door while the ancient-looking computer took ages to flicker into life. After what felt like days watching the circle of doom go round and round as the computer struggled to connect to the internet, I was able to put Bethlehem into the search engine and then sat back and waited again while the computer listed the search results.

"Bingo!" I said. "There is another Bethlehem! Two, in fact!"

Molly bounded over to me. "Osky, you're so clever!"

"Thanks." I did feel pretty clever. "Look, there's this one, a tiny farming village in the county of Carmarthenshire, Wales, and also this one – it's a hospital in London."

Molly scratched her head. "Do you think they went to the Wales-y one or the London one?"

"I think if you were a pregnant lady, you might pick the hospital-Bethlehem over the tiny-farming-village-in-the-Tywi-Valley-Bethlehem. And it is in the east, that might count for something. We'll just have to check at the post office tomorrow and hope for London. It's closer and we don't have much time."

I then typed *turkey sanctuaries near Chipping Bottom, Hampshire* into the search bar, and sat back for twelveteen hundred minutes while the results loaded.

"There's a hedgehog rescue place, and a cat and dog shelter, both over thirty miles from here. Oohhh, THIS! Turkey Cottage! No...hang on, that's a holiday let." I scrolled through a bit further. "No, there's really only Lady Asster's donkey sanctuary up round the back of George Budwell's place."

Molly looked a little bit delighted. "We shall just have

to keep Grandma in the bathroom then until the end of the holidays and then we can smuggle her home in Colin."

"We can't take her home, Molly! Where would we keep her?"

"In my Wendy house in the garden, of course!"

"Molly, we have to find somewhere to take Grandma now. It is not fair on her to keep her cooped up in the bathroom with the Angel Gabriel, Balthazar and Steve. She's going to Lady Asster's donkey sanctuary and she will be happy there, I promise."

I said that all very confidently, but I wasn't at all sure if a donkey sanctuary would even take a turkey. I decided that we'd just have to turn up and hope for the best. Surely they'd be animal lovers? They wouldn't turn Grandma away, especially at Christmas.

Before the family supper, I went to check on the bathroom posse to see how things were going and to tell them about my two-step plan for the following day. Two steps made it sound quite doable, I decided, even if it didn't feel like it.

Step 1 was to take Grandma to the donkey sanctuary early in the morning.

Step 2 was to then head straight to the post office to find out whether they'd sent Mary and Joseph to Wales or London.

I found Steve and Grandma curled up together asleep in the bath. Meanwhile the Angel Gabriel and Balthazar were giving each other the silent treatment, having fallen out quite spectacularly over a closely contested game of Uno.

I told them that we would set off extremely early the following morning and that it was likely that we would be out for quite some time and we'd need to work as a team as we had a big challenge ahead of us, so they had better sort out their differences or I'd be very, *very* disappointed with them. I confiscated their cards and left only once they'd promised they'd behave.

Grandmother was the last down to supper that evening. She entered the room with a big sigh and looking incredibly glum. She didn't even comment that Aunty Marigold was talking on her phone at the dinner table or that Molly was dressed as a firefighter.

"Are you alright, Mummy?" Uncle James asked.

"You seem quite out of sorts."

"I'm just so terribly disappointed about the nativity, darling. I rang St Augustus's to see if we might perform there, but they were adamant about putting on their own little 'show'." She did the air quotations when she said show. I don't think she thought that highly of the St Augustus performers.

"What a shame," Mum said, although she didn't look too disappointed about it not going ahead.

Aunty Marigold put her phone away. "Oh, that is a shame."

"Do you know, I heard that last year they played popular music? Appalling, really, that anyone should be 'Rocking Around the Christmas Tree' in the house of God," Grandmother said with a grimace.

"Fret not, Minty old girl! All is not lost!" Grandfather said. "For Patryk and I have formulated a cunning plan!"

Grandmother shot a confused look in Patryk's direction. "Whatever do you mean?"

"We have decided to take this year's nativity outside."

Grandmother raised an eyebrow. "Outside?"

"Patryk is our resident architect-extraordinaire and it so turns out that having such talents in the family is very useful indeed! If he can knock up a skyscraper, he can knock up a stage in no time, isn't that right, Patryk? I'm sure we could do it in a day!"

"I think that if we all pull together, we could build a stage on the village green, no bother," Uncle Patryk said. "Us actors, Araminta, always find a way to share our art."

"Marigold's a dab hand with a hammer, aren't you, love?" Uncle James said.

"It has been known," Aunty Marigold said.

"Good-oh!" Grandfather nodded enthusiastically. "The weather is set to be fine, so I thought why not? String up some lights, put out some chairs. You know, I think it would make it even more special. I'm sure some of the parishioners would be happy to help too. They wouldn't want to be denied a performance from Araminta Cuthbert-Anderson, now, would they?"

Grandmother didn't say anything for quite some time.

Then she burst into tears and said, "Oh, I think it would be wonderful! And, Patryk, call me Minty."

Grandfather placed his hands on top of hers. "So do I! Well, that's settled then. Work begins tomorrow! We're going to be terribly busy, but I think we can do it!"

Molly jumped up on her chair and shouted, "AND IT CAME TO PASS! THERE WILL BE A NATIVITY!"

I couldn't help myself from adding a "Hallelujah!"

Grandmother's smile dropped. "Christopher, please get your child down off the furniture immediately. She really is such a clamberer. I've never known such flagrant disregard for antique furnishings."

"Come here, you little monster." Dad picked Molly up and plopped her onto his lap.

Aunty Camilla stopped rubbing her belly for a moment and said, "This doesn't mean I'm getting on the back of that danger-donkey though."

"You're a Cuthbert-Anderson, for goodness' sake. Saddle up, Camilla!" Grandmother said.

Aunty Camilla did a massive eye-roll, tore off a bit of her bread, stuffed it in her mouth and said, "Fine, whatever."

"Thank you, Camilla," Grandmother said, with quite a triumphant nod of her head.

"This nativity is going to be the best there ever was," Grandfather said, "except for maybe the real thing – that would take some beating!"

If it actually happens, I thought. Because if I didn't find Mary and Joseph, then the real nativity wouldn't be coming to pass and that *would* be a problem. I supposed, at least, with everyone busy constructing a stage, it meant our chances of disappearing unnoticed to go on a hunt for the holy mother and her husband had definitely increased.

Oh, what fun it is to ride

on a sit-down lawnmower

That evening just before bed, the thought of having only two days left to find Mary and Joseph was weighing heavily on my shoulders. The possibility of failure was too unbearable. With no Christmas story, there would be no Christmas, which would mean that, for so many families, there would not be a chance to make special festive memories. No Christmas stories of their own. There would be no Christmas games of Monopoly ended prematurely by a sleeping grandmother, no families resting their bellies in front of the telly, no Christmas cards sent reminding people that they were loved.

I was kind of glad of the distraction when Margaret

brought our costumes for the nativity and demanded we try them on before lights out, so she could make any alterations if necessary.

I picked up my shepherd's costume, including the full-on bushy brown beard that I was very pleased about, for the others to see. "Looks very biblical-shepherdy, don't you think?" It was actually remarkably close to what Steve had on when we found him, minus the mud and sheep poo.

Hugo nodded. "What else would you expect from Grandmother? She probably had the cotton imported directly from Nazareth."

Molly was thrilled with her gold-trimmed white gown, golden halo and actual feathered wings. When Fenella put on hers, Molly stopped flapping about the nursery and said, "Wow! Fenella, you make a very beautiful angel. The beautifullest. I think the Angel Gabriel would be very jealous if he saw you."

Fenella blushed and tried not to smile, then said, "And you look like an absolute darling too, Molly. A real dream."

Hugo wriggled into his angel robes, then said, quite miserably, "How do I look?"

Ridiculous was the honest answer. "Very angelic."

Fenella giggled. "Oh, you can be a good sport when you want to, Hugo!"

"Well, it's for Grandmother and by extension Grandfather too, if you follow his logic."

He strapped on his really quite enormous wings and spun around to look at his back in the mirror. "I do wish I could have been a shepherd. I think I'd look good with a beard."

Molly put her hand on his arm and nodded sympathetically. "I understand, Hugo. I really wish I could have been a sheep."

He looked at me hopefully and said, "Swap?"

"No chance."

"No, I don't blame you." He sighed and flopped down on his bed.

I grinned at him. Something had changed up in the nursery that night. I guess that's what happens sometimes, when families come together for a common reason. That's what Christmas is all about, really. Family and loved ones.

After we had been down to show Grandmother what we looked like and she had instructed Margaret to take Molly's gown up a tad and to give my beard a bit of a trim to "neaten it up but not too much because while he still needs to look like a hard-working shepherd, he also has to appear as one worthy of being called to the bedside of Our Saviour", we were sent back upstairs to bed.

When I was in bed, I set my watch alarm for 6 a.m. Tomorrow would be the twenty-third of December, which I worked out gave us forty-two hours until midnight on Christmas Eve – not long, not long at all.

Our first job was to deliver Grandma to Lady Asster's. Then we were heading to the post office. And after that, hopefully off on the trail for Mary and Joseph. I knew it was going to be a big day. But it turned out to be much bigger than I could have ever predicted.

A few hours later, I was woken by my alarm buzzing on my wrist. I got up and quietly dressed and tried to ignore the sicky-nervous feeling in my stomach. I gave Molly a gentle shake, then told her to change out of her jim-jams and that I would meet her in the downstairs bathroom as soon as she was ready.

Quietly, I crept down the main staircase, along the corridors and out the back door. The cold air hit my face. The sky looked grey and heavy, like it might actually try to snow, but I reminded myself that it never snows at Christmas. The coldness sent a surge of excitement through me as I raced across the yard to fetch the ride-on lawnmower. I climbed up into the driver's seat and drove it round to the back door, hoping that no one inside would hear the engine. I parked up and opened the back of the trailer, ready to load Grandma onboard.

Inside the bathroom, Molly was swooshing her cape about and explaining to three very confused faces who Mothgirl was.

"Come on," I said, "we need to get going."

We had all just grabbed a corner of peacefully sleeping turkey and were carrying her across the carpet when the door burst open and Hugo said, "What are you two up to in here?!"

My stomach dropped all the way down to my ankles.

"I can explain!" I blurted out, although I had no idea how to even start.

Luckily, I didn't have time to make any excuses, because Fenella looked from me to Molly to the Angel Gabriel, then to Steve and Balthazar and finally to the sleeping turkey cradled in our arms.

That's when I saw the terror register in her eyes. She obviously wasn't a turkey fan.

Her mouth opened wider than I knew a mouth could go and she screamed. Boy, did she scream.

It was a very high-pitched and very loud scream – the kind of scream that makes your ear canals itch.

All the loud screaming startled Grandma Turkey out of her slumber. She clocked Fenella and Hugo and decided they were an immediate threat. Reacting to all her turkey-survival instincts, she launched herself at the twins in a flurry of squawks and feathers.

Fenella didn't hang around long.

She charged off down the corridor, stumbling as she went, and Hugo took up chase behind.

"I'd appreciate it if you didn't mention this!" I shouted after them, then added a hopeful, "Please?"

"Uh-oh!" Molly said. "I think they saw us."

"Possibly, Molly, quite possibly," I said. "Quick, let's get out of here before the rest of the family show up."

Grandma was running up and down the corridor, *gobble-gobble*-ing like crazy. I tried to catch her, but it just sent her into more of a flap. Luckily, Shepherd Steve cracked out his turkey-herding skills. He stared her right in both eyeballs which, because her eyeballs are on either side of her head, was quite something to witness.

Then Steve held a hand up and said, "Be calm. Sit."

And she did! I wondered if that would work on human Grandmother.

Then Steve said, "Walk on," and she got up and

walked down the corridor and GOT HERSELF IN THE TRAILER!

"That was amazing!" I said, as we all clambered aboard the mower. Mind you, what do you expect from the world's most famous shepherd after Babe the sheep-pig?

I turned on the ignition, just as a light switched on in one of the upstairs windows. I slammed down my foot and off we shot across the garden, heading for the fields to Lady Asster's before anyone had a chance to stop us.

It was a bit of a squeeze on the mower and I had to steer standing up as Molly was perching on the driver's seat, which was not ideal. Especially when her Mothgirl cape flapped into my eyes. I couldn't see where I was going and, during all the panicky screaming and grappling for the steering wheel, I accidentally knocked a lever which lowered the grass cutters.

When I managed to get Molly's cape out of my face, I tried to pull the lever back up, but in all the chaos, and because of my very powerful muscles, I accidentally yanked the thing clean off.

But I pressed on bravely under the light of the still-present moon, cutting a very neatly-mown strip behind us and showering my passengers with grass cuttings.

Once we'd come to the end of the second field, we had to drive up the lane at the back of St Bartholomew's to get onto the fields that led to Lady Asster's donkey sanctuary. The blades made a really loud noise when we hit the stones and I was pleased when we were mowing the grass again.

A few fields later, we pulled up outside a building with a big smiling donkey hanging over the front door and I switched off the engine. It was only then I realized I was quite out of breath from all the exhilaration.

The Angel Gabriel climbed down from the trailer, spat out a load of grass cuttings, staggered about on wobbly legs, then said, "That was horrendous! Quite possibly the worst experience of my life."

Molly jumped down, landing on two feet, and with her hands on her hips examined the place. "Yes, this is brilliant! Do you like it, Grandma?"

Grandma Turkey did not respond in any way as far as I could tell, but Molly said, "She says she loves it!"

I told the Angel Gabriel and Balthazar and Steve to hide behind some bushes so they wouldn't be seen and Molly and I would deal with the rest of the turkey delivery on our own.

They were just out of sight when the owner of Lady Asster's donkey sanctuary – who I was later surprised to learn was called Shenice Rose and not Lady Asster – came out of the front door, looking quite baffled, which I suppose is understandable.

"Well, this is a surprising sight," she said, wiping her muddy hands down her overalls. "A boy and..." Shenice tilted her head and looked Molly up and down.

"Mothgirl!" Molly shouted, punching her fist in the air.

Shenice smiled but still understandably looked a bit bewildered. "A boy and *Mothgirl* on a lawnmower at seven thirty in the morning!"

I think she was even more surprised when Grandma poked her head out from the trailer.

Not-Lady-Asster looked from Grandma to me then back to Grandma, then to me again. "What am I seeing here?" She pushed a stray curl out of her face and I could see she had kind eyes. It gave me hope that she might listen to what I had to say.

I gave her what I hoped was a reassuring smile and said, "Let me explain."

23

Last Christmas I gave you my
turkey

"So, here's the thing," I said as I climbed down from the lawnmower. My feet were all fizzy from the vibrations of the pedals, but I think I managed to walk over to her with confidence.

"Lady Asster," I said, because I thought that was her name at the time. "We are here to ask for your help, two animal rescuers to another. We have a turkey here—"

"The most magnificent turkey in the whole world," Molly interrupted.

Not-Lady-Asster said, "My name is Shenice Rose, not Lady Asster, and I can very clearly see you have a turkey, but I'm a little unsure what that has to do with me."

Before I could continue my carefully considered, convincing and compelling speech on why she should look after Grandma Turkey, Molly blurted out, "We want her to live with you so she doesn't..." She put her hand over her mouth and whispered so Grandma wouldn't hear. "...get a lemon stuck up her bum and eaten."

"You want me to take this *turkey*?" Shenice Rose said, like it was the most ridiculous suggestion in the world.

"Yup," Molly said. "Will you? Her life depends on it."

"But this is a donkey sanctuary," she said, gesturing to the giant donkey sign.

"Is a turkey really that much different to a donkey?" I asked.

Shenice Rose gave me quite the look.

"Pleeeeeeeeeease," Molly said, clutching her hands together.

"You want it to live here, with me?" Shenice Rose said again.

"No, I really wanted her to live in my Wendy house at home, but Oscar said no, so here will have to do," Molly said.

"A turkey, here?" Shenice Rose said again.

267

"Yes, a turkey here." I tried not to sound impatient, but I still had to make a trip to the post office and locate Mary and Joseph before anyone missed us. "So what do you say?"

"I'll tell you what I have to say, young man," came a voice from behind me, "and that is: what in the world is going on here?"

"Dad?" I knew it was him before I even turned around.

He had a look on his face that I would not describe as particularly festive, especially in comparison to his Christmas jumper with the flashing baubles on it. Grandfather was with him. He didn't look quite so furious, more bemused.

"How did you know we were here?" I asked.

"How did I know you

were here?" Dad spluttered. "We followed the line of freshly cut grass, that's how! Fenella and Hugo woke the whole house up, shouting about you attacking them with a turkey! Is that true?"

As if on cue, Grandma did a very loud and very proud "GOBBLE-GOBBLE".

Dad jumped back and yelped. "Good Lord, it is! What on Earth are you doing with a turkey?"

"What turkey?" Molly said innocently. "I don't see any turkey."

Grandma took this as her cue to really confirm her existence and flapped down and started *gobble-gobble*-ing in between us.

"THAT TURKEY!" Dad shouted.

"I think they want me to take it in here," Shenice Rose said, *finally* getting it.

"What?" Dad said.

"Is that the turkey we won in the raffle?" Grandfather said. "The one that went missing, young Molly? The one you named...Grandma?" The way he was speaking, with this twinkle in his eye, made me think he wasn't cross, but rather enjoying himself immensely.

"Oscar ran her over with the lawnmower but she's

269

alright now. She really is a very good turkey. She's very well trained. She does everything Steve tells her. Isn't that right?" Molly said, giving Grandma a stroke on the head.

"Who?" Dad said.

"Nobody," I said.

"Extraordinary," Grandfather said.

"Oh please say you'll take him, Lady Asster," Molly continued. "I really just think you should say yes. Because I don't want her to die." Then she looked at Grandfather and said, "I don't want anyone to die," and then she burst into tears. Which I don't think anyone was expecting.

"Oh, Molly." Dad picked her up and took off her Mothgirl eye mask and wiped the tears from her eyes. "My poor, kind, wonderful girl."

"Er, I'm the one who did the driving," I said, thinking I might perhaps get some of the praise. The look on Dad's face quickly told me that my thinking was wrong on that.

Shenice Rose didn't know quite what to do, what with all the crying and begging that was going on, so she just stood there eyeballing Grandma and Grandma just stood there eyeballing her back.

270

"I'll pay," Grandfather said, "for the turkey's room and board. Handsomely."

"You'll do *what*?" Dad said.

"It would appear that this turkey's future is very important to my grandchildren and therefore I find myself in the puzzling situation of it being very important to me."

Molly said, "Oh, Grandpops, you are a hero!"

But Shenice Rose still didn't say anything. She looked quite shell-shocked, to be honest.

Then she shook her head, laughed, threw her arms in the air and said, "Fine! I can't believe I'm agreeing to this, but the turkey can come and stay. It is Christmas, after all. Bring her round the back, I know just the place we can put her."

Molly leaped out of Dad's arms, wrapped herself around Shenice Rose's legs and said, "You're my hero and you are a very nice lady."

And Shenice Rose looked down at Molly's tear-stained but smiling face and said, "And you are very heroic too, but I wouldn't expect anything less from Mothgirl."

It was a nice moment, and then reality hit me three times over.

The first time was when Dad said, "Right, back to the house with the both of you. We need to have a long conversation about your behaviour. Your mother was beside herself with worry when we realized you'd gone off joyriding on a lawnmower. You two are going to be grounded until next Christmas if your mother has her way and, at the moment, that is a strong possibility."

The second time was when I realized that we would have to abandon the Angel Gabriel, Balthazar and Steve in the bushes.

The third was when I realized that our quest to find Mary and Joseph suddenly looked like it might not be happening.

As Dad put Molly into the trailer, and Grandfather was fixing the lawnmower lever, I glanced over at the bushes and mouthed "*Stay there*" and prayed that they had seen. I'd have to figure out a way to get back to them. And fast.

As Grandfather revved the engine and shouted, "Tally-ho!" I knew there was no way I was going to stop now. There was just too much at stake.

24

'Tis the season to be

a little bit untruthful but for a very good cause

The whole way back on the lawnmower I grew more and more concerned about the Angel Gabriel, Balthazar and Steve being out in Chipping Bottom on their own. They just weren't built to cope with the modern world. Balthazar ate potpourri, for goodness' sake. I needed to get back to them and soon.

Hugo and Fenella were waiting at the bottom of the stairs when we were marched into the house by Dad. They looked very smug, probably because they knew we were about to get the rollicking to end all rollickings. To be honest, any other time, I would have been really worried about getting a full family telling-off so close to

Christmas, what with presents hanging in the balance. But the only thing I could think about was that if the baby Jesus wasn't born where and when he was supposed to be born, there would never be ANY Christmas ever again for ANYBODY, and maybe no ME if I didn't think of a way to get Operation Save Christmas back on track.

"We're back!" Dad called and everyone else piled into the entrance hall, probably desperate to find out what we'd been up to.

"What on Earth were you doing keeping a turkey in the downstairs bathroom?" Mum shouted. "Have you seen the mess in there?"

"I simply cannot believe it!" Grandmother said. Then she looked us up and down, put her hand on her forehead and said, "I simply cannot believe it!" again.

Hugo stepped forward. "Who were those people, the ones with you in the bathroom?"

"What people? There weren't any people," I said, just as Molly said, "The Angel Gabriel, Steve the shepherd and Balthazar the wise man."

Mum frowned. "Oscar, what's going on?"

"There wasn't anybody in the bathroom with us," I lied.

Look, what can I say? I lie to my parents. I could say that I don't, but I do. All the time. About all sorts. Homework (rarely done), what I ate at school (always cheesy chips and *never* the healthy option), what I'm doing (computer games not reading), if I've brushed my teeth (sometimes), if I've washed my hands after going to the loo (if I remember).

This lie, to save Christmas, was more important than any other one I had ever told. So it's a good job I had had so much practice. "They must have been imagining it... you know, in all the turkey commotion."

I looked at Hugo, begging him not to say anything else. His brow crumpled, but his mouth stayed shut.

Aunty Marigold, who for once didn't have her mobile welded to her head, said, "Poor Fenella is traumatized. She has a phobia of big birds. What do you have to say for yourselves? I think you need to apologize to her and Hugo."

"We're sorry for attacking you with a turkey?" I said uncertainly.

Fenella sniffled. "It's okay."

"Well, I should think so too," Aunty Marigold said.

"It was an unusual course of action," Grandfather

275

said, taking off his hat and putting it on the stand, "but I assure you the children undertook this mission for altruistic reasons. Isn't that right, Oscar?"

I hadn't the foggiest idea what "altruistic" meant, but I said, "Oh yes, very altruistic reasons," because it sounded good.

"They were acting in the turkey's best interests," Grandfather said.

"What about my best interests? I was traumatized!" Fenella said, very dramatically.

Mum said, "I'm sure you'll be fine. It was a turkey not a Tyrannosaurus rex."

"Yeah!" Molly said. "And no one's going to stick a lemon up your bum and eat you for their Christmas dindins, are they, so pipe down!"

Fenella's mouth dropped open for a moment while she struggled to find something to say. When she did, she wiped her nose on the back of her sleeve and said, with a slight smile on her face, "I suppose that's true."

"I think now might be a good time for us all to take a moment to calm ourselves. No one has been hurt – in fact, a turkey has been saved. I suggest we breakfast," Grandfather said. "There is much to be done today, we

276

have a stage to build! And a show to put on, for tomorrow is Christmas Eve!"

"And these two have a bathroom to clean," Dad said.

"That's right," Mum said, then she jabbed her finger at me and Molly. "And you'll be staying in there until the whole room sparkles."

No, we won't, I thought. First chance we got, we'd be off locating the others and saving Christmas. I'd already lied, and I'd do whatever else I needed to do to get things sorted, and if that meant not cleaning the bathroom, that was just an added bonus. Although, I might have to ask the Angel Gabriel if he could sort me out with some kind of pardon too when I was talking to him about the favour I needed for Grandfather.

After breakfast everyone else got really busy with the building of the stage and sorting out things like music and lighting, which gave me a chance to quickly grab some food and stick it in my bag. Molly and I were then sent to the bathroom with a bucket of cleaning products, to go and tidy up.

Mum said she'd be back in an hour to check how we

were getting on and that she hoped that while we cleaned we would think about what we had done wrong.

Molly said, "I promise I won't not ever attack my cousins with a turkey again."

Mum crossed her arms. "Just get the job done and I expect exemplary behaviour from you both from now on. Do I make myself clear?"

She did make herself clear, but I still had no intention of following her instructions. She can't have been more than halfway down the corridor when I cracked open the tiny bathroom window and Molly and I made our escape.

When we got to the stables, I discovered that someone had taken the keys out of the mower.

"Oh bottoms!" I said. "No transport." Molly would never be able to keep up on foot. I put my hand on her shoulder and said, "Molly, I'm afraid that you might have to stay here. It's a long way to Wales or London, and I don't think you can manage the distance."

Molly swooped her cape behind her and stood with her hands on her hips. "Yes, I can, Osky." She pointed over my shoulder. "On him."

Little donkeys,

plural?

I gave Donald a look up and down, then said to Molly, "Are you sure about this?"

"I am very, very sure. The surest!"

I helped her up and said to Donald, "You be careful with her."

He gave a snort of agreement.

Molly gave him a little kick to get him started and shouted, "I LOVE YOU, DONALD!" then off we went, out into the fields and down the track that led to the village.

Once we were there, we tied Donald up to a tree and hurried to the post office.

Tricia Pennyworthy, the woman who owned the

place, was only just opening up when we arrived, which meant we hadn't actually lost any time with the whole turkey-saving quest. Tricia let us in when we told her it was a matter of the utmost urgency and Molly flashed her felt utility belt at her and said, "Don't make me use this on you."

Tricia fiddled with her hearing aid and said, "Yes, precious?"

"Have a pregnant lady and a man been in here asking for directions recently?" I asked before Molly could get too Mothgirl on her.

She looked at me quizzically. "Why yes, lovely couple. Seemed a little lost though and kept talking about a donkey. Two days ago, I think. Asked me where Bethlehem was, of all places!"

My heart leaped up to the back of my throat where my tonsils used to be. "And what did you tell them?"

"I thought they were pulling my leg to start with, but they were quite insistent. I checked on the computer and found two places called Bethlehem! Who'd have thought it? Not me!"

"Wales and the hospital in London?" I said.

"Yes, that's right!"

"And where did they head for?"

"London, but they wouldn't get a bus. Seemed terrified at the suggestion. Said they were going on foot. Not your usual ramblers, in my opinion, but I gave them an Ordnance Survey map so they could take the country roads. You know, I've been awful worried about them."

"So they're walking to London?" They had a two-day head start on us. I began to worry that we wouldn't catch them up.

"I suggested they should stop a night, what with the woman expecting. Looked ready to pop to me. Oh, that Lady Cuthbert-Anderson was in here at the time, she recommended some lovely B&Bs on the route."

Wow, Grandmother had inadvertently sabotaged Christmas by helping Mary and Joseph on their journey to the wrong Bethlehem. Did not see that one coming.

Tricia wrote the names of the B&Bs down on a piece of paper and sold us an Ordnance Survey map which cost me all my pocket money. We thanked her and legged it just as she started to ask why we were so interested in a couple of people on a walking holiday.

I popped Molly back on the donkey and then we headed for Lady Asster's, praying that we would find an angel, a wise man and a shepherd still hiding in a bush. I know God has a lot of prayers to listen to, but it's possible he might have heard mine, because they hadn't moved an inch since we'd left them.

"I bring tidings of great joy," I announced, expecting some sort of praise, for the style of my announcement at least.

But the Angel Gabriel popped out from the shrubbery and said, "What took you so long? Time is running out!"

"Steve and I are ever so weary and hungry," Balthazar said.

I broke off a bit of Mum's Christmas cake, which I'd brought in my bag, and got them up to speed, showing them the map and where we should be heading while they ate.

"We shall have to move swiftly. It is a long way," Balthazar said. Then he sighed. "Oh, for a camel or a horse!"

"We don't have horses," I said, looking towards Lady Asster's, "but I think I know where to borrow a whole platoon of donkeys."

Several moments later, I'd written a quick note to Shenice Rose informing her that we (obviously I didn't put my name to it) were on an important mission and that we would return Wonky, Sequin, Zipper and Kong back in one piece at the end of the day. Hopefully. I didn't write the *hopefully* bit, but I certainly thought it.

We saddled up and tore across the fields in search of Mary and Joseph, with a new-found confidence that comes from galloping on a powerful beast. When I say *tore*, I really mean plodded. And when I say *galloping,* I really mean plodding. And when I say *powerful,* yeah, I really mean plodding again. Whoever had named Zipper was having a laugh.

But anyway, it was better than walking.

Uphill and down dale, across streams and through woods we travelled, with me trying my best to navigate us towards the east. It's not easy to read an Ordnance Survey map while riding a donkey, with what still felt like a ton of Christmas cake in a rucksack on my back, but I hoped beyond hope that I'd be able to lead us to Mary and Joseph. Surely they couldn't have got too far, what with Mary being so pregnant? But I worried that people were probably much more hardy back then and used to walking great distances. They could have gone miles.

Molly tried to keep spirits high by singing a never-ending version of "Little Donkey".

But in reality, it only added to the weird tension that comes from being on a mission of such magnitude, racing against a very fast ticking clock, but yet clomping along on the back of a very unmotivated ass.

It was around lunch time when we came to the first B&B on the list. I dismounted and then, walking like a cowboy because my bum was more than a little bit sore, I went to the door with Balthazar while the others hung back. I imagined a boy turning up on his own might draw too many questions.

I knocked and a man with a big red nose with white hair sprouting out of it opened the door a little way, stuck his head out and said, "We're full," and closed it again.

I knocked again.

Mr Red Nose opened it and said, "What?" quite impolitely.

"I'm sorry to disturb you, it's just we're trying to find some people. Did a pregnant lady and a man come by here?"

"Yeah, yesterday evening and I told them what I told you – we're full. Sent them on to Marjory's place a few miles down the road. You could try there."

My heart lifted. If they'd been here only yesterday

evening it meant that we were catching up with them!

"Thank you, thank you so much!" I said and then I added a "God bless you!" because I was feeling so joyous.

Old Red Nose pulled a face then shut the door on all my joyousness.

I knocked on the door again.

"One more thing, could I borrow your phone please?" I knew I needed to ring home in case Mum and Dad were panicking about where we were.

"Okay," he said, "but it'll cost you a quid."

I rummaged around in my pockets and didn't find anything – I'd spent all my cash at the post office. "Give me a second," I said and ran back over to the others.

"Does anyone have any cash?" I asked.

Balthazar found a two-pound coin in the back pocket of Dad's cords. He really didn't want to let go of it though, because he said it was, "so beautiful". I pretty much had to prise it out of his fingers.

I went inside and handed the cash over to Old Red Nose and he gestured at the phone. I took a deep breath and dialled the house number.

Somebody picked up. I swallowed hard, said, "Hello?" and wondered how on Earth I was going to explain where Molly and I were and what we'd been up to.

"Hello?"

"Look, I don't want you to get angry but—"

"Oh, it's you. Where are you? I thought you were cleaning the bathroom?"

"Hugo?"

"Obviously."

"Is everyone mad at us? Are they worried?" I asked.

"What are you talking about? Everyone is out on the village green building the stage. They've been there all day. There's been a terrible ruckus with that Mrs Tadworth – she tried to get the whole thing cancelled due to planning regulations or something. Started dismantling the stage herself at one point. Anyway, everybody has been terribly busy. Reckon they'll be out there late into the night. Nellers and I have been stuck here all day with Margaret, keeping out of the way. Hang on, where are you?"

"So *nobody* has missed us?"

"No, what's going on?"

My parents' lack of attention to our whereabouts was worrying, yet useful. "Look, Hugo, I'm going to ask you a big favour."

"You can ask, doesn't mean I'll say yes."

"It's really important, I need you to cover for me and Molly. When they get back later, make out that we're already in bed asleep. And then make more excuses until we get back."

"Where are you?"

"I can't say."

"Intriguing. When will you be back?"

"In time for the nativity, definitely. I think. So, will you cover for us?"

"Hmm. Look, are you okay? I know you're up to something and Fenella and I have agreed to keep quiet about what we did or didn't see in the bathroom, but if you're in some sort of trouble, you had better say."

"I'll give you all my Christmas presents."

"I don't want your Christmas presents, I want to know where you are and if you and Molly-Pops, I mean Molly, are okay."

"And I've got about thirty-six pounds in my coin tin at home, you can have that too."

"Look, I don't want anything. Just tell me what's going on."

"I can't, not now, and you wouldn't believe it even if

I did. Just please, cover for us. Trust me, things are fine
– well, they will be, I hope."

"Okay, I'll cover, but it's Christmas Eve tomorrow –
you'd better be back for the nativity or I shall tell them
and insist they send out a search party."

"Thank you, Hugo. Honestly, you're brilliant."

"Just get back in time and, whatever it is you're up to,
be careful."

"I will be."

"Oh, actually, there is one thing you could do for me."

"Go on, name it."

"Right," I said, climbing back onto Zipper, who gave a
little huff. "What?" I said. "You're a donkey, you're born
for this."

He gave a little whinny, but he knew I had him there.

"So what did they say?" Molly asked.

"Don't worry, I've squared things at home, Hugo is
covering for us."

"Hugo?" Molly said.

"Yup. Let's just say, I'm sure he'll look very good in
his shepherd's beard."

26

Star of wonder, star of night

– nope, hang on, that's an aeroplane

We had some more of Mum's Christmas cake for lunch, then headed off in the direction of Marjory's place, that Old Red Nose had said was just a few miles down the road. I think he and I have a different definition of *few* as it took us several more hours of plodding and the sun was weakening in the sky when we finally arrived at the B&B, and we almost missed the sign because it was getting so dark. I checked my watch. It was just past four.

Balthazar and I went to the door and the others hung back with the donkeys again. I knocked and was quite surprised when a man with a nose as big and hairy as the last one's answered.

"Marjory?" I said.

"No! I'm Brian. Are you taking the mickey?"

"It's just it says *Marjory* on the sign. Look, we were wondering if—"

Before I could finish, Brian said, "Sorry, no room," and closed the door again.

I knocked. Again.

He swung the door open quite forcefully. "What? I'm in the middle of *The Muppet Christmas Carol*."

"Sorry to interrupt you," I said politely, "we just wanted to ask you if a pregnant lady and a man stayed here. It's *very* important."

"As a matter of fact, yes. Left this morning. Nice couple. Sent them on to some holiday lets a few villages along – Bert's Bungalows. They're kipping there for the night."

"When you say *few* how many do you mean?" I asked, but he'd already closed the door.

We went back to the others and I pulled out the map. The Angel Gabriel lifted up his hat a bit to provide a bit of light. "Now listen up, everyone, the plan is to head as far as we can towards this village where I believe Mary and Joseph are staying tonight. Hopefully we'll be able to get to them before they head off tomorrow morning. That will give us a day to get back to Chipping Bottom, get them transported back to the proper Bethlehem, get us to the nativity and, most importantly, save Christmas and also me. Everybody understand?"

They all nodded.

"Good, let's get going then."

We trudged on for a few more hours, but as the night crept in darker and darker, it became difficult to find our way through the fields and lanes and woods. It was getting cold and Molly had long stopped singing and was now asking, "Are we nearly there yet?" every three minutes. I didn't have the heart to tell her that we might not even be heading in the right direction.

"Fear not," Balthazar said, pointing to the sky. "We shall follow that star, for it is the brightest of stars and I believe it will lead us to our destination...although it is leading us very quickly. Trot on, Sequin, we must make haste!"

"That's not a star, that's an aeroplane," I said. "That's why it's going so fast."

"A what?"

"Like a bus in the sky," I said.

"I do not know this *bus* of which you speak," Balthazar said.

"It's what people use as transport."

"Oh, like a camel."

"Yes, an aeroplane is like a giant metal camel with wings that flies in the sky," I said a bit sarcastically.

He thought about it for a bit, then said, a little forlornly, "In that case, we shall not follow that star."

But mere moments later he pointed skywards excitedly again and said, "We shall follow that one instead."

"Again, that's not a star, it's a satellite."

"I do not know this *satellite* of which you speak."

I thought about explaining a satellite, but the aeroplane had been tricky enough. "Let's just stick to using the map, shall we?"

"Perhaps I could be of some assistance?" the Angel Gabriel said and removed his flat cap.

I was once again startled by the magnificent light of his halo.

I knew Molly was too, because she let out an appreciative, "WAH WAH WOO WAH!"

294

But Steve, who was right next to him, yelled, "MY EYES! MY EYES!"

With the Angel Gabriel now leading the way, we carried on our journey a little longer, but when Molly almost fell off Donald because she was struggling to stay awake, I knew we'd have to stop. We found a barn, tied up the donkeys and gave them some water to drink. Then we bedded down in the hay, hoping to get some shut-eye. The insides of my legs were humming with soreness from having been on Zipper all day.

If you one day decide to take up donkey-riding, I recommend that you build up slowly so your bum has a chance to get used to it.

After some more of Mum's Christmas cake, which everyone agreed tasted better the more you got used to it, we decided to try and get some sleep. Molly fell asleep immediately and Balthazar and Steve passed out not long after we had settled down, snoring in unison, but I couldn't drift off.

There was a still quietness about the night, but my thoughts were anything but calm.

There was a question, a *favour* kind of question, I wanted to ask. The one about Grandfather. The one that

I'd been carrying with me ever since I'd first met the Angel Gabriel.

"What happens?" I said, looking out through a large hole in the barn roof at the billions of stars that twinkled in the dark night sky overhead. The heavy clouds that had threatened snow earlier had gone and it was a crystal-clear night.

"What happens?" the Angel Gabriel echoed.

"You know, when you die?"

"Ah, the big question. The one everyone wants to know the answer to."

"So," I said, my voice shakier than I'd expected, "what happens?"

"That is not for me to say. It is a journey that all people must take themselves, when the time comes." He paused and smiled at me. "And my, Oscar, what a journey it is."

"It's good then?" I couldn't imagine that was true.

"It is part of life, Oscar. Do you find life good?"

An image popped into my mind of our family nativity rehearsals. Uncle Patryk leading an imaginary donkey and Aunty Camilla's horrified face at being told she'd have to ride a real one. Molly bellowing her lines and Mum and Dad trying not to laugh at her or at Grandmother's Angel Gabriel dramatics. Fenella and

Hugo giving stellar performances even though they didn't want to be there. And Grandfather. Looking on at us all proudly, his eyes twinkling whilst shouting *Bravos*. "Yes," I said, "I really do."

The Angel Gabriel's eyes sparkled. "Yes, so do I. Never understood the appeal myself – before now, that is."

"Ah, but that's because you'd never had a foot spa or played Uno before."

He looked at Molly, wrapped up in her cape and asleep in the hay, and then his eyes settled back on me. "It's more the people that make it so good though, don't you think?"

I nodded and his words made me feel a bit warm in my ears, then gave me a lump in my throat. "Absolutely."

"Sadness and joy sit very close together, Oscar. One cannot exist without the other."

And although I felt that, I didn't understand why at the time, so I just nodded and we sat looking at the stars in silence for a while. My head was spinning as I desperately tried to think of a way to ask what I knew I needed to ask.

I scratched a stick on the ground so I didn't have to

look at the Angel Gabriel when I spoke. "Sometimes, my dad gets favours from people he works with," I finally said, very quietly. "You know, like a perk-of-the-job type thing."

"I can't help your grandfather, Oscar. I am very sorry, but that is not how it works."

I didn't look up. I just tried not to cry as the disappointment billowed through my body. "I guessed that. I'm sorry, I just thought I'd ask."

"Do not ever say sorry for love, Oscar. It is the most magnificent thing there is and it shines out of you, brighter than any halo."

It wasn't the answer I'd wanted, but there was something about the Angel Gabriel's words which calmed my thoughts and sleep finally found me.

27

There wasn't no room, no room at the Inn

– should have stayed at Bert's Bungalows

It was beyond cold in the barn overnight, and even though we were buried under lots of hay to keep warm, with only our heads poking out, we all woke around two on Christmas Eve morning, unable to sleep because we were frozen to the bone. I honestly thought my face might fall off, it was *that* cold.

Steve suggested we try the method he uses out in the fields when it gets a bit chilly. I wasn't sure about it at first, but Zipper actually did make a rather effective but very hairy hot-water bottle when I cuddled up to him, and we all managed to get a few more hours' kip.

We woke again a little later that morning, our breath still puffing out in clouds in front of us. Through the hole in the roof I could see that the thick grey-white clouds had returned and with them they had brought a chance of snow.

"I really, really, *really* hope it does," Molly said, vibrating with excitement. "Do you think donkeys like sledging, Osky?"

"I have no idea if they do, but I hope it doesn't snow – it might slow us down."

"Then I hope it snows when we're back with Mum and Dad and Grandfather and Grandmother and all the others," Molly said. Then her chin quivered. "I miss them, Osky. I love them all so much and I really love Christmas and I just want everything to be okay. It will be okay, won't it, Osky?"

"Yes, Molly," I said. "It will all be okay."

It had to be.

I checked our position on the map and once we had all done our morning wees in the bushes, we set out in the darkness towards Bert's Bungalows, hoping that we would find Mary and Joseph there.

Everyone was pretty tired, except Molly, who must have some kind of built-in switch, because she is either on or off. She started up a rousing rendition of "Little Donkey" once more, which she powered through despite the chorus of groans from all the other donkey riders.

By my reckoning it was going to take a couple of hours to get to Bert's. It was an anxious trek. I worried that Mary and Joseph might be early risers and that they would have set off at the same time as us, making it impossible to catch up with them before it was too late. We needed to pick up speed.

I decided we needed to give our donkey-mobiles a bit of a gee-up.

"Now, Zipper! Now, Donald! Now, Wonky, Kong, Sequin!"

On Balthazar, on Molly, on Gabriel and Steven!"

To the top of the field, beyond that brick wall!"

Now dash away! Dash away! Dash away, all!"

My rather genius and, I think, motivating poem, did not result in the injection of pace that I was hoping for. Where's a flock of flying reindeer when you need them?

And so we continued to trundle along as the clock ticked down and our bums grew sorer and our hopes got weaker. Even a field of extremely fluffy sheep failed to raise a smile from Steve.

My mind bounced between how important it was to continue on our mission and how terrifying it would be facing Mum and Dad when they found out I'd not cleaned the bathroom, done a runner with Molly, borrowed a pack of donkeys from Lady Asster's and set off across the countryside without telling a grown-up what we were up to. Well, not a grown-up born within the last millennium.

Yeah, that was going to be *some* conversation.

But eventually, when the sun was just beginning to rise in the sky, we spotted the village we were looking for and our spirits lifted.

"Is that Bert's Bungalows yonder, in the East?" Balthazar called out. "For I see a sign which says *Bert's Bungalows* and it is in the East!"

"Hallelujah!" the Angel Gabriel said. "I believe it is."

I gave Zipper a kick, hoping that we might gallop down the hillside with a little more enthusiasm, but Zipper seemed completely unmoved by the sighting of our destination.

We tied the donkeys up in the car park of Bert's holiday lets and this time we all went to knock on the door of reception. I'd already clocked the FULL sign, so when Bert answered the door, I was ready.

"Look, I know you're full, but we just want to ask a question."

Bert stretched and yawned, then he rubbed his hand across his stubbly chin, gave us all a very strange look and said, "Rough night? You lot don't smell so fresh."

He didn't look or smell particularly sparkly either, but I guess we might have smelled worse – using a donkey for a duvet probably hadn't given us the most lovely of scents.

"Did a pregnant woman and a man stay here last night? They might have told you they were walking to London," I said.

"Oh, those two! Yeah, and they told me more than that! Called themselves Mary and Joseph and they were off to Bethlehem to be counted! Hilarious, they were. Think they must have been doing a walk for charity or something. I let them stay in Bert's Banging Bungalow number three. Gave it to them for free, what with her expecting and it being Christmas Eve today and all."

"I am sure you will be rewarded for your kindness," the Angel Gabriel said.

Bert blushed. "Well, it's just what you do, isn't it?"

"Are they still here?" I said.

"Dunno. They may have dropped their key in the box. I don't mind people checking out like that, see. Stops me having to get up so early."

We all watched as he opened up a box just outside reception. He held up a key with a large wooden block attached to it. He turned it over so we could see. The number three was printed on the side. My heart sank.

"Yeah, guess they left already. Sorry, couldn't tell you when. Hold on...what's this?"

This time he held up a couple of very old-looking coins.

"Looks like they paid after all," I said. "You should probably get them valued, they look pretty old."

We left Bert studying the coins and climbed back on the donkeys.

"Hopefully they haven't got too far," I said.

"Don't worry, Osky, our wonder-donkeys will get us to them in no time!" Molly said.

"Molly, they are hardly wonder-donkeys. I mean,

they are steady and reliable, but I wouldn't say they'll get us anywhere quickly."

"Shall I ask them to go faster?"

"Molly," I said, a little wearily, "you can't talk to donkeys."

And then Molly went, "EEE-AWWW eee-AWW-AWW. EEE-ee-AWW!" and I swear to the Big Guy himself, the things only began to trot!

I would NEVER have believed it was possible, but as the evidence was now trotting happily beneath me, it's hard for me to deny that it happened.

We crossed over a track, along a bridleway, across another field and then onto another track which hugged the side of a small wood.

And that's where we saw them.

Two figures, determinedly making their way to Bethlehem.

The completely wrong Bethlehem, mind you, but it was still quite a wondrous sight to behold.

28

O' Holy Night

"**L**ook! It's them!" I said, and I suddenly felt very emotional and I wasn't completely sure why. Maybe it was the lack of sleep, or my bruised bum, or maybe it was just something about them that made my insides feel...hopeful.

The sound of donkey clip-clops must have alerted them to the fact that someone was coming up behind them. They swung around and the Angel Gabriel took off his hat so his halo beamed bright and said, "Mary and Joseph, I bring glad tidings of —"

But before he could finish, Mary said, "Oh, finally, we were wondering when one of your lot would show up.

Now, which one of you is going to tell us what happened?"

"The Angel Gabriel blasted you into the now future with all his big powers which he sometimes uses for smiting and you all went KABOOM!" Molly clapped her hands above her head. "And then you all landed in a field in Chipping Bottom with a BUMP and an ARGHHHH and Osky and I have had to collect you all, a bit like Pokémon, so we can send you back to the olden times where the sheep aren't as fluffy and Jaffa Cakes don't exist!"

No one said anything for a moment. Mary and Joseph stood there, looking at us all in complete bewilderment.

"You've got to admit, Gabes," Balthazar said out the side of his mouth, "she really is beating you in the impressive announcements stakes."

The Angel Gabriel climbed down off the donkey named Kong and walked towards the holy couple, arms outstretched, and said, "Come on, let's get you home, for you have the most wonderful job to do."

And they both nodded, like they just *knew* it was true.

Mary climbed on the back of Donald the donkey with Molly, and Joseph hopped on Zipper with me and off we trampled back to Chipping Bottom. It was well past midday and we had a good few hours of travelling ahead of us. I wanted to get back in time for Grandmother's nativity and I was hopeful the return journey would be quicker because we had a better idea of where we were heading.

"I thought Bethlehem was in the East, the way we were headed," Joseph said as we set off.

"I guess it is, but waaaaaaay more East than the Bethlehem you guys were headed to."

"Now, tell me, where exactly did you land when you arrived in Chipping Bottom?" the Angel Gabriel asked. "It is of the utmost importance we return you from whence you landed."

"Where was it, love?" Joseph called over to Mary.

"The sign said *Village Green*."

"Right," I said. "It is possible that when we get there, we might find a tiny bit of an audience."

It had begun to grow dark again when we finally arrived back in Chipping Bottom, after a long and tiring journey. But as we clip-clopped down the main street towards the green, we saw the village had been lit up by string after string of lanterns. Grandfather and the others had done a great job of getting things ready. Patryk's stage was really quite something.

The villagers of Chipping Bottom were all sitting under the star-studded sky and my entire family were standing by the stage, dressed in their costumes, looking like they were in the middle of what Grandfather would call a "heated discussion" – I thought it was probably about me and Molly. From up on the stage, the vicar was trying to assure the congregation that the nativity would be starting presently.

Hugo was the first to notice the procession of donkeys travelling towards them. He pointed at us and shouted, "Look! They're here! I told you they'd be on time!"

Everybody – my family, Mrs Pennyworthy in her *Single and Ready to Jingle* jumper, Mr Chandra, Mrs Tadworth, the whole audience – all turned around and gasped when they saw us. I suppose the sight of five donkeys, the real Mary and Joseph, a shepherd, a wise man, the Angel Gabriel, Mothgirl and me coming up the street was quite gasp-worthy.

The vicar made a very strange noise down the microphone that went a bit like, "AAA ooooo errrr whaaaa?"

Mrs Tadworth stood up and said, quite hotly, "What on Earth is going on?"

Shenice Rose jumped from her fold-up chair and shouted, "My donkeys!"

And Mum and Dad ran towards us, shouting, "Our children!"

Grandmother climbed up onto the stage, snatched the microphone and said, "Would you all please give us a moment, while we see to a few...er...technical issues...

which I am very pleased to see have arrived." She smiled, then she cried a bit, then she smiled again, and I think even though she had called me and Molly *technical issues*, I could tell she was genuinely pleased to see us. She really looked quite magnificent, standing up on that stage in her brilliant white angel cloak, giant wings, long blonde wig and tinsel halo.

The Angel Gabriel frowned. "Who's she supposed to be? Not me, is it?"

When Mum and Dad got to us, I couldn't quite read the look on their faces. I think, if pushed, I'd describe it as a furious-joy.

"What's going on, Oscar? Where have you been?" Dad asked, as Molly and I climbed off our donkeys. "Who are these people? Hang on, are they wearing my clothes?"

Uncle James and Grandfather dressed as the wise men and Aunty Camilla and Uncle Patryk dressed as Mary and Joseph and Aunty Marigold as an innkeeper and Hugo and Fenella as a shepherd and an angel, all spilled out onto the stage to get a better look at what was happening.

Mum grabbed me and Molly into a fierce hug, then said, "Oscar, explain yourself immediately!"

But I didn't have to, because the Angel Gabriel climbed down from Kong and removed his hat and his halo lit up the space around him with the most wondrous glow. Then he unfurled his enormous white wings and they sprang out behind him in the most magnificent way.

There was a lot of gasping again – understandable.

Dad's mouth opened and closed more times than I could count and Mum just stood there, staring, her eyes as wide as the moon.

The Angel Gabriel placed his hand on my shoulder and smiled, then walked over to Mary and helped her down off Donald. And then with Joseph, they proceeded down the walkway between the seats, with Steve and Balthazar following behind.

I think this is when some people started to realize exactly who had rocked up on the donkeys with us.

Some people stayed absolutely silent – way too stunned to speak. But I could make out Tricia from the post office saying, "Is that...no, it can't *really* be them!" And I heard George Budwell asking his wife, Nancy, if Balthazar was the guy who fell through his roof.

This is when the vicar really lost his cool. One moment he was standing at the front of the stage, his eyes and mouth competing to see which could open the widest, the next he was very much horizontal.

"The vicar's fainted," Molly said.

I guess it's a big day, meeting your heroes.

We all walked up onto the stage where the rest of my family were still standing and formed a semi-circle around the unconscious vicar.

"Whatever is going on?" Mrs Tadworth shouted across a now completely silent congregation. "Why are there two Marys? Why are there two Josephs? Why are there so many donkeys? Is that child dressed as a super *moth*, for heaven's sake?"

But nobody paid any attention to her; they were too enthralled by the unbelievable events that were unfolding in front of their eyes. Dad and Mum ran up onto the stage and looked like they were about to say something, but I shook my head and put my finger to my lips.

The Angel Gabriel had something to announce. Something important. Something wonderful.

"I bring glad tidings of great joy!" the Angel Gabriel began. "For a child will be born in a manger in Bethlehem and he shall be the son of God!"

Grandma pulled a face and muttered something

about that being her line, but it couldn't detract from the sense of awe and wonder that had filled the air in Chipping Bottom that Christmas Eve night.

The Angel Gabriel looked at me and nodded. "And so…"

"And so," I said and nodded back.

It was time.

They were going back.

And I felt such sadness and joy all at the same time. Sadness that they were going, but joy that I'd known them in the first place. I looked over at Grandfather and I understood what the Angel Gabriel had said the night before in the barn.

Then the Angel Gabriel raised his hands above his head, and a light brighter than any I had seen before lit up the whole of Chipping Bottom and probably most of Hampshire, causing even more gasping.

Once it had faded, I looked around the stage and saw they had gone.

No one said anything. Silence and utter bewilderment pulsed through the night air.

Then the vicar came round and said, "What…what… happened?"

I felt Molly's hand in mine and she whispered, "We did it, Osky! We really did it!"

But she spoke a moment too soon, because suddenly Uncle Patryk shouted, "Hey, you're not my Camilla. Where's my Camilla?"

A flash of light lit up the sky, again. Everyone gasped. Again.

And the vicar fainted. Again.

The Angel Gabriel was back, with my stunned-looking aunty.

"Sorry," he said, "took the wrong Mary. Now that could have been a *really* catastrophic mistake."

Aunty Camilla blinked a couple of times, then said, "Eeeee, urrrrr, whhaaaaaaa?"

Angel Gabriel pulled a face. "Don't worry, she'll be alright in a bit."

"You also forgot Donald," I pointed out.

The Angel Gabriel looked at him, snuggling up with the other donkeys. "I think we can leave him here. He'll have a nicer life at Lady Asster's, of that I'm certain."

I grinned at him. "He up there okay with everything? Still have your angel-ing licence?"

"It's in the balance, but I think I'll be okay if I get the

actual Mary back where she should be."

"I'm glad I met you," I blurted out.

The Angel Gabriel then spread his wings wide and announced, "And I am glad I met you, Oscar Anderson. And now I shall leave you, on this most joyous of occasions: the Christmas you saved Christmas!"

I think that was his best announcement yet, to be honest.

Although Mrs Tadworth, who looked really quite deranged by now, ruined it a bit by shouting, "WHAT? WHAT? WHAT?"

The Angel Gabriel looked across the stunned congregation and seemed to realize that he may have overdone it a bit. Again. "Hmmm, probably best than none of you remember any of this."

"None of us?" I said.

"Except you and Molly. You are both special. It must be why I appeared unto you."

There was another flash of light and the Angel Gabriel and the actual Mary were gone.

Properly this time.

I can't tell you how long we stood on that stage before somebody snapped out of the communal trance – it was definitely a while.

319

It was actually Mrs Tadworth who rose from her chair again and said, "What happened here? What happened here?"

No one seemed quite sure, but when I said, "Quite possibly the best nativity performance that anyone has ever seen," they all went along with it, and I made my very slightly dazed family join hands in a line and take a bow.

And even though no one could quite remember what had happened, they all knew they had definitely experienced something pretty wondrously spectacular, so we got a standing ovation.

Grandfather turned to Grandmother and said, "You did it, Minty, my angel, you did it!" Then he looked over at me and the rest of the family and said, "My heart has never been more full."

And neither had mine.

As the applause continued to ring out across Chipping Bottom village green, one voice rose above the others.

"Osky!" Molly shouted, tugging at my arm. I turned to see she was cross-eyed and pointing at her nose. "Osky, is that…?"

I laughed. Of course it was.

"Yes, Molls, it is," I said. Because there, on her little button nose, was a single, perfect snowflake.

We both looked upwards and from the sky above us more snowflakes began to fall. It started gently at first, but soon more and more flakes were fluttering from the sky.

"Osky!" she shouted. "It's SNOWING!" Then she spun round with her mouth open, trying to eat the softly-falling flakes. "I told you it could snow here on Christmas!" she squealed. "I knew it would, if I believed hard enough! I knew it would!"

"Oh, how marvellous!" Grandfather said, and I completely agreed.

Mum scooped Molly up into her arms and spun her around and Dad looked up at the sky, then grinned at me. "Do you believe it, champ? Snow!"

"Yeah, I believe it," I said. I believe in a lot of things now – especially the magic of Christmas.

I'll Be Home For Christmas,

well Barlington Hall

29

When the envelope arrived the following December with its red wax seal, we all – even Mum – knew what our answer would be to the invitation inside, even though we had a ready-to-go excuse as Molly had just had her tonsils taken out.

The week before Christmas, we waved Granny Roberts and Norma off as they got in the taxi taking them to the airport for their Caribbean Christmas cruise, then we got into Colin and Dad programmed the satnav to take us to the Hampshire in South England, not the one in America. And we headed off to Barlington, me with Mum's building-block of a Christmas cake on my lap and Molly singing "Little Donkey" until she, thankfully, fell asleep.

I woke her up again when we turned into the driveway leading up to Barlington Hall. My whole body was full of excitement. I was so looking forward to seeing everybody, but I was sad too, that Balthazar, Steve and the Angel Gabriel wouldn't be there this time.

Uncle Patryk, Aunty Camilla and their new baby, Feliks, met us on the front steps with Grandmother.

"Oh, Cathy, I see you brought a cake!" Grandmother said, gesturing to the cake box Mum was staggering up the steps with. "We never did find out what happened to the last one."

"I hope it's okay," Mum said.

"I'm certain it will be wonderful. Now, your grandfather is upstairs resting," Grandmother said, pulling me and Molly into a hug.

"You smell nice," Molly said.

"Thank you, Molly-Pops. And what is it you are supposed to be today?" she asked, stroking the ears of Molly's costume. "Some sort of bear?"

"No, silly, I'm a donkey," she said, then did a couple of *EEE-AWWW*s for good measure.

I had a moment, up there on the steps, when I remembered Grandfather being all tangled up in the Christmas tree lights the year before and I had to stop still for a second because I thought I might cry. But I thought about sadness and joy, and a smile found its way to my face instead of tears.

Aunty Camilla and Uncle Patryk had moved in to help Grandmother when Grandfather had grown more ill. It had been Grandmother's idea. Apparently she had said, "To have a family member like Patryk about the place who is so good at fixing things would be a blessing." But we all knew she just liked having him around. He was a bit of a hero in her eyes for building that stage. He also had plans for Barlington Hall which would help keep the place in the family. It turned out that Grandfather and Grandmother were struggling a bit to pay for the house. They hadn't wanted to say anything, but when Patryk found out, he came up with an idea. He was going to open it up to the public for weddings and events. Grandmother hadn't been completely thrilled, but Patryk had won her over. I overheard Dad talking to Uncle James about it – I think they were both delighted that Uncle Patryk was willing to do what they couldn't, and that he'd seen Barlington as something worth saving.

Uncle James, Aunty Marigold and the twins arrived not long after us. Once we had dumped our bags in our room, Molly, Fenella, Hugo and I ran straight to see Grandfather.

My heart clenched when I saw him. He looked much frailer and smaller than when I'd seen him in the summer, but when he saw us a huge smile stretched over his face, I remembered the man who would slide down the banisters and I couldn't help but beam back.

"I thought you'd arrived," he said, pushing himself up in bed. "It sounded like a herd of huffalumps running up my stairs."

"I'm not a huffalump," Molly said, "I'm a donkey!"

Grandfather laughed. "Why, yes! I see that now! And what a fine donkey you make."

"I wish we were doing the nativity again this year," Molly said. "Look how good I can *eee-awww!*"

Molly *EEE-AWWED* about the room, while the rest of us tried our best not to laugh.

"*Bravo!* A fine portrayal of a donkey," Grandfather said. "But you know, I'm glad that it is Mrs Tadworth's turn. I don't think anyone could put on a better nativity than the one we did last year."

"It's bound to be completely boring," Fenella said, plopping herself down on the foot of the bed. "I think we should boycott it."

"Well, I insist you don't," Grandfather said, a mischievous smile twitching on his lips. "See, your Grandmother and I have been talking about that and we might just have a plan to liven things up."

"You have?" I said.

"Yes, but it is to be a top secret operation, understand?" Grandfather said, tapping the side of his nose.

Hugo grinned. "Whatever it is, we're in."

We all huddled in close as Grandfather went through the details.

Once he'd finished, I said, "And Grandmother knows about this?"

Grandfather nodded. "She certainly does."

"It's going to be A-MAZING!" Molly said and did a little donkey kick.

"I wish I could be there to see it," Grandfather said.

"You can't come?" I said quietly.

He shook his head, then took a breath and patted

the bedcovers. "Come, sit."

Fenella scooched up on the bed to make space for Molly on one side and Hugo and I sat down on the other.

"My dear grandchildren, I wish to speak honestly with you, if I may?"

"Of course," Fenella said, taking his hand.

"You all know I have been unwell for a while and the doctors believe that it is very likely that I am coming to the end of my life."

I felt the hotness of tears welling up behind my eyes, but before they could fall, he said, "And what a wonderful life it has been. I want to tell you, while I have the chance, that you four and now dear Feliks, are amongst my greatest joys. You have brought me more happiness than I could ever have possibly imagined. I am terribly lucky to say that I sit here with you, a very happy man."

I don't think any of us knew how to respond so we sat there in silence until Fenella blurted out, "But, Grandfather, I just can't bear the thought of you not being here!"

"But I will be here, in a way," he said. "Each of you will carry a little part of me inside. No one is ever truly gone, when there are people around to remember them."

328

He smiled kindly. "Now, enough of these glum faces. Something *I* can't bear is the sight of you lot looking sad. Besides, I believe you all have a plan to put in motion."

There was a knock at the door and Margaret came in with Grandfather's supper.

"Sorry," she said, "am I interrupting something?"

"Not at all," Grandfather said, "We have definitely not been planning a secret nativity operation, have we, children?"

"We definitely-wefinitely have not!" Molly said.

30

God rest ye merry gentlemen

It was four days before the Christmas Eve nativity, and with Grandmother's help, we had all the plans sorted for Grandfather's secret mission. We were out carol singing at the Chipping Bottom villagers and were still laughing at Mrs Tadworth's reaction to our rendition of *Joy to the Worm*, when Margaret came running along the street, her scarf flapping behind her and looking very white-faced.

"Your Ladyship," she said. "It's Lord Cuthbert-Anderson. I fear it is time."

I think her words hit everyone with the same enormous impact and it took a moment for anyone to respond. Grandmother gave a small nod then said, "Right, then we must get back to him at once."

The walk back to Barlington Hall passed in a blur. Dad and Uncle James had their arms around Grandmother and the four of us cousins held hands the whole way.

We pushed open the large front doors of the house, and together, we climbed the stairs up to Grandfather's room. There, we gathered around his bed. Grandmother sat in the chair and placed her hand on Grandfather's chest and said, "I'm here, Reginald. Your Minty's here."

His eyes were closed and he was too ill to speak but Dad said he would still be able to hear us, and we took our turns to say goodbye. We all told him how much we loved him and how much happiness he had brought us.

I wanted to say more; there was so much more inside of me. But it's hard to put the love you have for someone into words. Words can never do it justice. I just had to believe that he knew.

Grandmother tried desperately not to cry when she said, "I have loved you so very much, Reginald. Thank you for your humour, your patience, and your love. And thank you, for sharing your life with me."

And then Molly reminded him, in case he was

worried, that we definitely wouldn't flush him down the loo, as she'd kept the large cardboard box in the garage very safe.

Everybody did a little confused frown after she said that, but no one questioned her about it.

We knew that it would be the last time that all of us would be in the same room, and we sat alone yet together with our thoughts and our feelings and our memories for a man we all loved. Memories of sliding down banisters and riding on lawnmowers and of the warmth of his laugh. I don't think I've ever felt joy and sadness so close together within me, before or since.

I barely noticed the very light knock on the door. Dad got up to answer it.

Grandmother did not take her eyes off Grandfather for a second; she just sat there, her hand on his chest.

Margaret stepped into the room, unsuccessfully blinking back tears. "The doctor is here."

"Please, tell him to come in," Dad said.

A moment later, someone said, "Lady Cuthbert-Anderson?" and I felt a change in the room.

I thought I was imagining it to start with.

But that voice.

I knew that voice.

Slowly, I raised my eyes and I saw his face. I tried to say his name, but my mouth wouldn't form the words.

Grandmother looked up too and said, "You're not Reginald's usual physician."

"No, I'm afraid he is out of town, but I heard of your husband's condition and I wanted to make sure that he was well looked after."

"I don't think there is anything you can do," Grandmother said.

The Angel Gabriel shook his head. "Your husband is a very sick man. I'm afraid it is his time."

Grandmother nodded, then she lifted up one of my grandfather's hands and slipped hers underneath. She looked around the room. "If you wouldn't mind, I would like to have a moment with Reginald on my own."

"Of course," Dad said.

I felt my chin trembling uncontrollably as we all filed out onto the landing. The Angel Gabriel put his hand on my shoulder and we moved a little further away from the others.

"You can't save him, can you?" I said, already knowing the answer.

"No, Oscar, I can't."

I felt a flash of anger towards him. "Then why are you here?"

"Because you're my friend and I wanted to be here for you."

The sudden fury I had felt disappeared as quickly as it had surfaced. I didn't even know I was going to do it, but I threw my arms around him and clung onto him so hard. My family were probably wondering what I was doing hugging the new doctor, but I didn't worry about that at the time.

The Angel Gabriel rested his chin on my head and said, "I know it's hard."

"It is, but I'm so glad you're here." I stepped back, wiped my nose on the back of my sleeve and looked up at him through my wet eyelashes. "But are you allowed to do that? Just come down to see me? Does *He* know?"

The Angel Gabriel nodded. "I think *He* knows everything." Then he smiled. "Let's just say me being here is a perk of the job."

I let out a spluttery cry-laugh. "Bet the angels with the worms and the boulders don't get those kind of perks."

334

"No, probably not." Then he smiled at me and said, "It's going to be okay, I promise. People die, Oscar, but the love you have for them doesn't. It will still shine bright, brighter than any halo."

I gulped, then I nodded, and I knew it was true.

31

Everybody knows a Turkey and some Mistletoe,

Make the Season Bright

On Christmas Eve, we all dressed in our best and headed off to St Bartholomew's to watch Mrs Tadworth's nativity. There had been talk about not going, but we decided we had to – for Grandfather.

We bumped into Shenice Rose from Lady Asster's outside. She hugged us all and said what a wonderful man Grandfather had been. She also told us how Donald was still getting on brilliantly with the other donkeys, which was nice to hear. And then, when our parents weren't listening, she whispered to me and Hugo that everything was in place like we'd planned.

As we entered the church, the vicar said some lovely

things to Grandmother about Grandfather. And then, as he handed us our orders of service, he said, "Poor Vivian will have a job to top last year's. It was the most phenomenal thing – a performance that you experienced more than watched, if that makes sense?"

"Oh, you never know with these things, sometimes the most unexpected happenings occur quite out of the blue," Grandmother said, and winked at me. We hung back while our parents took their seats in a pew and Grandmother turned to Fenella, Hugo, Molly and me and said, "Are you children ready? You know what to do?"

We nodded, but before I disappeared to my position at the back of the church with the others, I said to Grandmother, "I wish Grandfather was here to see this."

She smiled and brushed my cheek with her hand and said, "Oh, Oscar, I imagine he's watching."

I gave her a kiss on her powdery old-lady cheek and hurried to the others, who were almost vibrating with excitement at the thought of what we were about to do. I spotted a little wooden nativity scene standing on a table at the back of the church. My eyes fell on Steve the shepherd and Balthazar and the Angel Gabriel and I smiled.

Silence fell over the church and Mrs Vivian Tadworth walked down the aisle to take her place at the lectern.

Baby Feliks let out a little wail which made Mrs Tadworth glare. Aunty Camilla started bouncing him up and down on her lap and Uncle Patryk made silly faces at him, which Feliks seemed to find funny.

Molly, Fenella, Hugo and I slipped out of our pew and sidled up to Shenice Rose. While we stood there waiting for the signal, I looked at the mischievous sparkle in the eyes of my sister and cousins, and I realized that Grandfather had been right about us all carrying a little bit of him inside us.

Mrs Tadworth tapped the microphone, opened her mouth and said, "Behold, what is that in the East?"

And right on cue, Molly opened the cage that Shenice had hidden behind the font and bellowed back, "It's Grandma Turkey!"

I don't think I've ever enjoyed a church service more. It was a chaos of feathers and squawking and screaming. Molly was jumping down the aisle EEE-AWW-ing loudly. Mrs Tadworth was hurtling about the place shouting at people to do something about "the feathery beast", whilst the congregation were jumping over pews to get out.

Mum, Dad and all my uncles and aunties stood frozen and looking absolutely bewildered by the scene that was unfolding. And right in the middle of it all, Grandmother sat laughing, her head thrown back and tears rolling down her cheeks. She turned to me and the others said, "Bravo, my darlings! Bravo!"

I grinned, then looked upwards and said, "There you go, Grandfather. Operation Nativity complete. Merry Christmas."

What Christmas Means to Me

While I wish I could have spent more Christmases with my grandfather, I am so thankful for the one we did have together. And he's been there, at every Christmas since, in the hearts and memories of the people who loved him. I only have to look at a set of Christmas lights to remember his sparkle, or the banisters at Barlington Hall to remember how much fun he was, or the ride-on lawnmower to remember his sense of adventure. And when I hear "Joy to the Worm", I remember his deep warm voice and I can almost feel it in my bones again and I am reminded of how much joy Grandfather did bring, to everyone who knew him.

Christmas will always be a very special time of year for me. It makes me think of turkeys and donkeys and Christmas cakes that could sink a battleship, and of carol-singing and of nativity plays. And of angels and wise men and shepherds – of friends. And of family. Those who are here, and those who are not. Christmas makes me realize how majestiful the world can be, because of the people in it.

So, this is the end of my story. The story of The Christmas We Saved Christmas. And it is up to you whether you choose to believe it.

But, whatever you decide, from my family to yours, have a very happy Christmas.

The End

Carry on the CHRISTMAS FUN with these FESTIVE ACTIVITIES

Design a Christmas Jumper

Steve the shepherd borrows various Christmas jumpers to disguise himself while he's undercover in Chipping Bottom.

Use the festive images as inspiration. Choose your favourites and copy them onto the jumper templates in pencil or black pen. Then use coloured pencils or pens to colour them in.

Or, draw your own designs from your imagination. Add a festive slogan too, if you like.

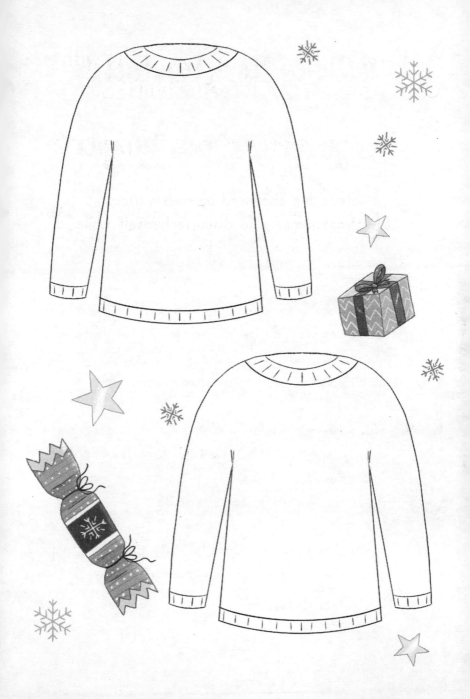

Nativity Story Fun Facts!

- The characters that the Angel Gabriel accidentally transports to Chipping Bottom were on their way to Bethlehem, which is part of modern-day Israel. Mary, Joseph and Steve can speak English to Oscar and Molly, but in real life they probably would have used the ancient Semitic language of Aramaic.

- Jesus probably wasn't actually born on 25th December. We celebrate in December thanks to Emperor Constantine, who chose the pagan festival of the winter solstice to mark Christmas back in 336 AD.

- The Guinness World Record for the biggest ever nativity scene was achieved in Alicante, Spain, in December 2020. Jesus, lying in his manger, measured 3.32m high, while Joseph was 18.05m tall.

- In the Philippines in 2019, the City Government of San Jose del Monte put on a nativity scene which involved 2,101 people!

Festive Funnies!

Here are some of our favourite Christmas jokes –
why not try writing some cracking ones of your
own?

What do you call an old snowman?
Slush!

How does Christmas Day usually end?
With the letter Y!

What goes "Oh! Oh! Oh!"?
Father Christmas walking backwards.

Knock Knock.
Who's there?
Tree.
Tree who?
Tree wise men!

Snowflake Decoration

Oscar's family make paper snowflakes to decorate
the church for their nativity performance.
Try making your own — you'll need a long
cardboard tube, glue and thread.

1. Press the tube flat then cut
off twelve loop-shaped strips.
Each one needs to be around
as wide as your finger.

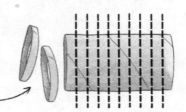

2. Open out six of the loops a
little. Glue two together, like this.

3. Glue on four more, so it
looks like a snowflake. Let
the glue dry.

4. Fold all the remaining loops in half, like this.

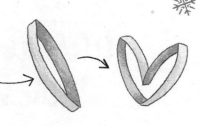

5. Glue both sides of each folded shape onto the snowflake. Let it dry

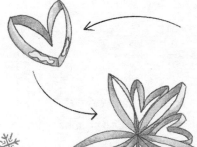

6. Tie thread through one of the loops to hang it up.

Celebrating Around the World

Just like the villagers of Chipping Bottom, people in different places all around the world have their own special ways to celebrate the festive season.

Poland

In Poland, families like Patryk's begin celebrations on 24th December, with a traditional supper called Wigilia. Wigilia begins when the first star appears in the sky, and all cooking and housework should be finished before then. Some people believe that what happens on Wigilia affects the new year to come – if you have a happy Wigilia, you'll have a happy year!

Ethiopia

Some say that the real Balthazar was a king of Ethiopia. In Ethiopia today, Christmas is celebrated on 7th January, and the celebration is known as Ganna. Most people dress in white clothing, and go to church, sing songs, play sports and eat wat stew with injera flat bread.

Iceland
In Iceland, there isn't just one Santa Claus, but 13 - the mischievous "Yule Lads"! Children will put a shoe on their window sill every night for thirteen nights, and on each one a new Yule Lad will visit and leave a gift.

Venezuela
In Venezuela, there's a tradition of people roller skating to church services over the Christmas period! The Three Wise Men deliver presents to children, and people celebrate with Gaita music featuring guitars and maracas.

Israel
In Israel, where Mary, Joseph and Steve the shepherd came from, most people are Jewish and so celebrate Hanukkah, the festival of light, around the same time of year as Christmas. A burning torch is passed from hand to hand to light the giant menorah at the Western Wall. People also eat fried food like donuts and potato latkes, as oil is an important part of the Hanukkah story.

Christmas Quiz

1) Which star could Santa use to navigate his way home?
a) The North Star
b) The Dog Star
c) Rigel

2) Roughly how many people were involved in the biggest ever snowball fight?
a) Eight hundred
b) Eight thousand
c) Eight million

3) Reindeers aren't deer.
   True or false?

4) No two snowflakes are alike.
   True or false?

5) When are the Twelve Days of Christmas?
a) December 1st – December 12th
b) December 14th – December 25th
c) December 25th – January 5th

6) In the nativity story, an angel announces the birth of Jesus to people working at night near Bethlehem. Who are they?
a) Guards
b) Thieves
c) Shepherds

6) C
5) C
4) True
3) False
2) B
1) A
Answers

Acknowledgements

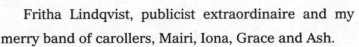

Thanks, as always, to my angel of an editor, the festively fantastic Rebecca Hill, and to Becky Walker and Alice Moloney for making this book a true celebration of Christmas. You are my three wise women.

Katie Kear, you are a gift of an illustrator – thank you so much for the joy that your work brings to the page.

Fritha Lindqvist, publicist extraordinaire and my merry band of carollers, Mairi, Iona, Grace and Ash.

To everyone at Usborne, I am so very grateful to be part of such a brilliant team.

Huge thanks to Will Foulger for his guidance on the religious themes in the story and to the whole Foulger family – Vikki, Joe, Iris, Jesse and Huck for being my first ever readers.

To the St Margaret's community, especially Helen Tait and Chloe Black who are always so supportive.

Thanks also to the many teachers, booksellers and librarians who have supported me – it is truly appreciated.

To my family, Andrew, William and Douglas who make my Christmases and all the days in between so special – thank you.